PLANETCRASH

MATTHEW BOUDREAU

Published by Level Up in the United Kingdom in 2020

Cover by Claire Wood

ISBN: 978-1-83919-311-8

www.levelup.pub

For my sister, who made me want to write

CHAPTER 1

Even a small space battle is an impressive thing to witness and this one was one of the largest in history. Both factions had brought all their might to bear for control of the star system Adonis. The homeworld and capital of the Cerulean Empire was here and if it fell the war would end tonight. The capital ships, the dreadnoughts, cruisers, and carriers of the United Front pushed ever closer, escorting their troop transports to the capital as the light of the local star shone off the gleaming, chrome armor plating of the fleet. A landing would almost certainly end with victory for the UF. It was common knowledge that the Ceruleans had lost the majority of their ground troops earlier in the war, during the disastrous failure of a surprise attack on UF territory. But, for now, they maintained their fleet superiority. It made this attack on their home system a terrible gamble for the UF and likely the decisive battle of the conflict.

I felt a twinge of regret that I was on the sidelines. I hadn't cast my lot with either faction and had been merely sent to observe and report. Today's battle would dramatically shake up galactic politics and my Kingdom, The Jovian Moon, wanted a head-start in the new order. I'd fought in my share of battles before, though, so it wasn't too straining to sit back and appreciate one as a whole, rather than through the narrow perspective and tunnel vision of a marine.

A series of explosions lit the side of the UF Dreadnought *Woodbridge*, expanding into a chain reaction throughout the

1

massive ship. The first dreadnought down of the battle. It had fallen to a sudden shift from over a thousand Cerulean single-seat fighters, each breaking away from its own dogfight to swarm on the dreadnought. It was a lion, killed by the simultaneous bites of innumerable mosquitos. The spectacle of the view of a dying dreadnought was second only to its implications: such a sudden disengagement from dogfights frequently led to the crippling or destruction of the fleeing fighter. It was an expensive way to bring down a capital ship, likely coming at the cost of hundreds of small Cerulean ships. It was a kind of maneuver reserved for a battle you didn't expect to win, directed out of a desire to bring down the enemy with you. Ceruleans had a larger navy to start with, which suggested that UF wouldn't be leaving this system with a single capital ship to their name. That didn't mean Ceruleans would win though. It would only take a transport or two to slip past the defenses and UF marines would capture the planet. It was difficult to defend a planet from transports, given the three-dimensionality of space. Unless you had enough ships to form a sphere around the planet, there would always be gaps. So the planet would likely fall. Barring a miracle from one side, the result here would be two destroyed Empires.

Immediately, I called my commanding officer. This was hot information.

"What've you got, Gee?" The response was instantaneous. He'd been expecting a preliminary report, but, caught up in watching the battle unfold, I'd forgotten to deliver. Until now.

"Ceruleans don't expect to win. They're fighting to collapse both Empires, not to survive." I paused. "Also, *Woodbridge* is down."

"*Woodbridge*…A dreadnought? Already?"

"Suicide attack from Cerulean fighters."

2

"Damn, okay. I'll pass it along. Call me again if another falls."

"Roger that."

I ended the brief call and turned my attention back to the battle. Now that was strange: a group of UF fighters had broken off from the main battle. Where were they headed? I strained to see the specks of light, far away at the other end of the solar system. I was loathe to take my sensors off the main battle for something that was unlikely to matter, but I was *curious*. I flipped the sensors to this small group for a split second, then back immediately. In that time I learned two things: first, they weren't ordinary fighters, they were a seeker squad, designed to detect stealthed ships. Second, they were headed towards the edge of the solar system, aimed almost directly at—*crap.*

Someone in the UF knew what was up. A carrier captain probably, with enough authority to order seekers around, but not enough to order a full retreat. They'd seen the Cerulean suicide attacks and come to the same conclusion that I had: UF and Ceruleans both would fall after tonight. Unlike me, however, the UF didn't want the rest of the galaxy to know this. So these seekers would be coming to kill me and the other observers that I knew must be out here, even if I couldn't see them. It was a war crime, actually, but it was the only hope the UF had of surviving the year.

The first step towards my own survival was to power down my ship. I overrode the safety warnings and got backup life support turned off as well. A good seeker ship would detect me from even the slightest hint of power flowing through my ship, so it all had to go. That left me with about five minutes before I ran out of oxygen and the ship became uninhabitable. I dashed to the small cargo area, the battle at the center of the solar system already forgotten. I was pretty sure there was a combat suit somewhere in here and the life support system on that had a

3

chance to evade the seekers' detection systems. A slim one, but it was better than leaving the ship powered up or my asphyxiating. There it was, at the very back of the hold. I pushed through the layers of accumulated junk to get at it. It occurred to me that I'd forgotten to set a timer to check the five minute time limit. Too late now.

I struggled into the suit, hoping I had enough time left. It couldn't have been five minutes yet, right?

I gave the suit its "power-on" command before even bothering to seal it. That would come next. Diagnostics flashed to life on my HUD, warning me of what I already knew: the suit wasn't sealed. No other issues, thankfully. I wasn't sure how long this suit had been sitting in my pile of junk, it might have worn out. The suit's computer started to automatically seal itself, but I overrode the command and sent it into low power mode, which shut down everything but life support. Every iota of power saved would increase my chances of evading detection and I could seal the suit manually.

Once I was in no immediate environmental danger, I returned to the helm. An explosion at the corner of my vision told me the seekers had found one of my fellow observers. A comrade in duty, if not in allegiance, even though we'd probably never met.

There was nothing else I could do until the seekers left. Trying to flee the system would only draw the UF squad to me. I decided I might as well try to do my job, whatever that would be worth without sensors. With the naked eye, there isn't much you can see of a battle from fifty AU away, no matter how big the battle is. I watched the explosions flash anyway. Was that a chain reaction, a downed dreadnought? On the left side of the battle, from my perspective. Which meant it was a Cerulean dreadnought. Or a UF one that was horribly out of position. I

4

had no real way to tell which. It could have even been a compact engagement between fighters.

My whole ship shuddered under an impact, presumably from the seeker ships. *You've got to be kidding! Are they toying with me, or just out of ammunition?*

A high-priority, short range distress signal forced its way through the overrides I'd laid on my suit. Grudgingly, I opened the message:

```
you almost had us, you sneaky weasel! guess
its not your lucky day, though, is it? >;)
```

I sighed. The seekers weren't messing with me and they probably weren't out of ammo either. No, it seemed that they'd found me from the sheer dumb luck of *crashing into me*. A moment later, my ship exploded.

```
GAME OVER
```

```
Create new character? y/n
```

The words flashed across my screen, in the usual orange and green of the *PlanetCrash* logo. It wasn't the first time I'd seen them, and it certainly wouldn't be the last.

I wasn't too upset, honestly. My character on this *PlanetCrash* server hadn't been a high achiever and was lagging behind most other serious players. Another server was opening up this weekend anyway, titled NA-22: the twenty-second official *PlanetCrash* server in North America. The start of a new server was a great event, putting every player and faction on the equal footing of having nothing, and it alleviated the sting of my character's death on NA-21. I'd been controlling a male avatar, for the first time, and named him Gart Gasper. Being Gart had been fun, but I was ready for something new.

Even so, I had school in the morning, so I logged off and returned to the boring, ordinary world of my real life.

5

CHAPTER 2

My *PlanetCrash* session had lasted longer than usual and I slept through my morning alarm. This left me in the unfortunate position of having to be woken up by my mother for school.

"Emily!" A shout from the kitchen. Better than when she came into my room, at least.

"Coming!" Acknowledging her was more important than actually obeying. I started to struggle out from under the covers anyway. I had to eventually, after all. Checking the clock told me I'd overslept by ten minutes. *Alas! I must compress my usually extensive morning routine.* The sarcasm of my internal monologue did nothing to alleviate my stress, but it still felt good. I grabbed a t-shirt and jeans at random and threw them on without meeting my own eye in the mirror. I wasn't running late anymore. The only thing I'd had to cut from my day was hitting the snooze button twice. *Not even the world of meat can stop me from accomplishing miracles!*

I tried to rush out the door, hoping my mother wouldn't notice the dark circles under my eyes. She'd gone to bed at a reasonable hour and was under the impression that I had as well.

No such luck: stealth had been a skill of Gart Gasper's, but it wasn't in Emily Wilson's toolbox.

Mom grabbed my arm on the way by. She was short enough that I, only sixteen, had already overtaken her height, but she still had a hell of a grip. "Just how late were you up?"

6

I briefly considered lying. She'd probably check, though. Part of the deal under which she allowed me to have a computer powerful enough to run *PlanetCrash* in my room was that I'd make my PlanetCrash profile, playtime statistics, and all available to her. I sighed instead. Hopefully, this way she wouldn't remember to ask if I'd done my homework…

"Five a.m."

"Five a.m.? Goddamn it, Emily!" She launched into the usual lecture. "There's so much more you could be doing, you could be doing better in school, you could learn an instrument…hell, you could do both in the time you waste on this. Do you want to throw your life away on this stupid game?"

I sat back and weathered it, nodding and mumbling "yes" and "no" when I felt it was expected. Sneaking a glance at the clock over her shoulder, I discovered that I was late again. I'd forgotten to account for *this* part of the routine.

Eventually she let me go. I trudged to the monorail, making no effort to make up time. I lost more, in fact: if you're going to be late anyway, you might as well minimize the part of the day that sucks. The Orange Line was busier than I was used to due to my delay, I was in the company of real commuters now and fewer high school students. I had to stand, but I preferred that. It wasn't a long ride and the city monorails were so smooth you almost never had to grab the handrails to keep yourself from stumbling. I'd been to Washington D.C. once, where they'd never managed to get the government to fund the switch from underground subways to monorails. It was dirtier, bumpier, and slower. I could almost understand why some people in D.C. still drove cars.

The ride to school was fifteen minutes, just enough time to mentally reset for school on an ordinary day. Running on ninety minutes of sleep was another matter. Much as I hated to admit that my mother might have been right, I knew today would

7

not be a good day for learning. Not that most days were, but usually you could hope. I descended from the elevated monorail station and into the street. My school was in the heart of the city, so only a block and a half of a walk remained after the ride. The walk was quick, even with the streets bustling full of commuters. The pathways been designed for a small city and Boston's population had exploded over the past twenty years. Estimates said we'd passed a million people by now, but no one would know for sure until the next census in 2050. I emerged from the crowd and pushed my way through the front door of my school. Half an hour late in total. I'd missed most of Chemistry. Not that it would matter to my final grade, since I could never wrap my head around the formulas and processes. This failing wasn't restricted to Chemistry, either. Things at school just never fit into my brain the way *PlanetCrash* did. I pushed through the door to the chem lab, mumbled what I'm sure Ms Carter would have assumed was an apology, and dropped into the nearest empty seat. She was merciful enough not to make a big deal of my late arrival, instead satisfying herself with a quick, disapproving look, never breaking stride in her discussion of redox reactions.

I wasn't awake enough to concentrate. I'd even been too tired to think to stop at a coffee shop on my way here. The only thing keeping me awake at all was thoughts of the character I'd build for NA-22 tonight.

Ms Carter pulled me aside after class. *Great. Another lecture.*

"You don't seem too well, Emily." My teacher had a unique accent from having been born and raised in London before living for years in Canada. The blend was interesting and unusual in Boston. "Are things okay at home?"

I blinked. I'd expected a lecture about *PlanetCrash*. Although, I suppose I was just being defensive: Ms Carter had no

8

way of knowing that I played. So she'd landed on a different possibility. My hesitation was confirmation enough.

"I should get to Algebra…" I didn't want to lie to her, but I definitely didn't want to tell the truth either.

She gave a small, sad smile. "Okay."

I ran for the first time that day and not because I was excited to learn Algebra.

The rest of the day passed in much the same way. I absorbed nothing in Algebra, avoided talking about my missing homework in History, and dozed off twice in English. All in all, school was long, boring, and exhausting. Not much different from usual, I supposed. It would have to do.

CHAPTER 3

After getting home from school, I immediately took a nap. The new server wouldn't be opening up until after eight p.m. and I wanted to be less overtired for it. Mom woke me again at six for dinner. She was chilly and I could feel the disapproval radiating off of her like a fog over ice. This suited me fine, though, as she seemed content to let her emotions remain cold, instead of exploding into an inferno of anger against me. That had happened before.

Dinner was silent and tense. I decided I'd have to make a big show of doing my homework at least until eight p.m.; hopefully that would mollify her a bit.

Dad came home only fifteen minutes after I'd started. Earlier than he had usually been these days: he was working ridiculous hours as his boss was retiring in a few months and he had his eyes on her job. Mom practically jumped up to kiss him, but even he could tell something was bothering her.

"Is everything okay?" Dad seemed genuinely concerned. Imagine that.

"We'll discuss it later, dear." Evidently Mom wasn't excited to jump back into an argument either. "For now, let's just have dinner."

He grinned. "That'll be just the thing."

Dad's presence at dinner defrosted the atmosphere a bit, but it was a far cry from warmth. He made a few attempts at humor, to push it over the boundary to lukewarm at least, but they were rebuffed by a stony silence from mom.

After dinner, as Dad did the washing up, I applied myself to my Algebra homework with a rarely achieved dedication. Never before had trigonometric functions made so little sense, but never before had I applied myself to them so furiously. The need to impress my parents enough for them to let me continue playing was paramount. Turns out the best way to make me care about school is to make it actually matter.

I finished Math in record time and moved onto History. My dad came in during the shuffle of books and sat on my bed. I turned from my desk to face him.

"Hey Dad."

"Hey Em." He paused. "I'm glad to see you working, but I think we need to have a chat."

I put down my pen. "Okay?"

"Your mother and I, well, we're concerned." *That's obvious...* "I know that school doesn't seem like a good use of your time, hell, I've never used Algebra since I was your age," he gestured at my textbook.

"Dad, I—"

"Ah-h-h!" He held up a hand to stop me. "Let me finish. I know you don't think you want to be some academic, or a doctor or whatever. And that's fine! But school isn't just about that. Doing well in school is about keeping your options open. I'm not asking you to get perfect grades. I just want you to do your best, okay sweetie?"

"Okay."

"Great! Now finish your homework." He smiled and left.

I almost felt guilty when I logged into *PlanetCrash* at precisely eight p.m. Almost.

11

```
Welcome back to PlanetCrash! Please select a
server.
```

After selecting NA-22, I got the usual message:

```
You do not yet have access to NA-22. Purchase
access? y/n
```

It was $10 to join a new server, but this was always worth it. I'd been playing for four years, since I was twelve, and they'd launched eight new servers in that time. Well, nine now, with NA-22. Ninety dollars for the best parts of the last four years of my life was an absolute steal. After reminding the server of my bank account information, I got to start creating my new character.

Character creation was always a dilemma. You couldn't change your character once you'd launched into the server, which meant you wanted to do it right the first time. On the other hand, every minute spent in the creator was a minute you weren't gaining items, cash, and exp: a minute spent falling behind the socioeconomic ladder of the new server. And with new servers, every minute counted. I decided to give myself two minutes. Remembering the near-catastrophe from last night's play session (or, rather, this morning's), I set myself a timer.

First, the important things. The name was key, but I'd already come up with that. I typed Emily Everston and saved it. I almost always used my real first name for my characters, but changed up the last to satisfy my love for alliterative names. Gart Gasper hadn't been named Emily, of course, as my first male avatar. The next most important thing was hair color. All of my characters were gingers. *PlanetCrash* has this beautiful shade of it you can put on your characters and I'm infinitely jealous that I don't have red hair IRL. Not that it would look as good on me as it always did on my characters.

I played a female character to match the name. Gart Gasper had been a fun stray into the world of manliness, but I never tired of good, old fashioned, kick-ass girl power.

Now onto stats. There were four stats associated with your character in *PlanetCrash*: Agility, Strength, Precision, and Manufacturing. Their effects were fairly self-explanatory: each point in Agility incrementally increased your move speed, jump height, and the like. Strength increased your movement speed, and most armor had a minimum strength requirement, so focusing points into it would allow you to wear better armor than players of equal level who hadn't. Since armor, and the shielding it provided, was the only source of HP for characters in *PlanetCrash*, you could get really tanky really fast if you dumped enough points in. Precision was an interesting one, as it affected your weapons more than your avatar. It didn't make them more accurate directly, as player skill was critical for that. Precision just made your weapons more favorable to accuracy: shotguns would have less spread in their shot; rifles less recoil; snipers would be steadier, and the like. A high-level character who'd focused Precision could make a headshot from across a solar system if the player behind the screen was skilled enough. Manufacturing was, in my opinion, the most boring of the stats and as a marine I was usually loathe to put a single point into it. It gave access to more advanced building techniques, that players could use to construct spaceships, weapons, and defensive fortifications.

Characters started with four points that you could distribute among these stats any way you liked and you gained an additional two points per level up. I put two in Agility, one each into Strength and Precision, and none into manufacturing. Being able to get around the battlefield quickly was a huge tactical advantage and one that I felt outweighed the benefits of better armor and accuracy.

13

The timer went off. Reluctantly, I finalized the new EE, a nickname which I could apply to all of my Emilys, and returned to the better half of life.

CHAPTER 4

The *PlanetCrash* tutorial was, unfortunately, required watching when you entered a new server. As if I couldn't already command a dreadnought-class ship in my sleep. At least, I was pretty sure I could. I'd never had an important enough role in a faction to actually try it. The thought reminded me: I needed to find a faction for this server. Thankfully, the tutorial wasn't taxing enough to prevent me from multitasking a bit. I pulled up the *PlanetCrash* forums in another window and browsed over the "Looking for Group" section.

Finding the right faction was key: factions dominated most of the galactic happenings on each *PlanetCrash* server. On the whole, factions were just a small group of IRL friends who wanted to play together. Above those were a collection of about a hundred "Kingdoms," factions that controlled a couple planets each and fought over anything that even looked like it might be valuable. Then there were the griefer factions: groups that just wanted to cause as much chaos throughout the server as they could and who knew that they couldn't stand against the Kingdoms without unifying. Eventually, and inevitably, a few Kingdoms would grow to the point where they could fend off the griefers and from there they would expand unchecked, forming the largest factions, the Ultimate Empires. The UEs would set up a protection business for the Kingdoms, keeping the griefers out of their territory in exchange for loyalty and combat support in the event of a war. War between the UEs was something else. It was fairly rare: across all of the dozens of *PlanetCrash* servers worldwide, only a few UE wars happened every year. Some servers had never seen a single UE war. But when they did happen, they were devastating. Kingdoms fell like mayflies, UE borders were dramatically redrawn, and the griefers did their best to ensure that the war lasted as long as possible. I'd only fought in one war myself, as a marine lieutenant loyal to a Kingdom sworn to a UE that had been invaded by another while our Emperor was on vacation IRL. I lost my best character in that war, but it was one of the coolest experiences of my life.

I scrolled through the faction recruitment page, trying to find one that suited me. I needed to find a Kingdom of perfect size: too small, and my experience would tempt the King to put me in command of something (eew). Too large, and I'd end up as a cog in a machine with no autonomy. Many kingdoms were present in every server, and, sure enough, I recognised their recruitment posts.

```
Join   the   Legion   of   Honor,   and   fight   for
justice      among      the      stars!     Contact
LoHRecruitment  (user page)  to find your place
in the Legion!

-LoHoffical
```

```
Resistance  wants  you!  We  ARE  NOT  GRIEFERS
(griefers: don't interact!!), we are DEDICATED
to  the  NOBLE  CAUSE  of  ensuring  that  every
Kingdom  is  free  from  the  eternal  protection
racket  of  the  UEs!  —dandan117  EDIT:  o  ya
almost forgot, see our forum page to join.

Are  you  an  elite-level,  dedicated  FPS  main?  Do
you  care  more  about  fighting  awesome  battles
and  winning  awesome  loot  than  the  empty  ideals
of  the  Kingdoms?  Are  you  not  enough  of  a  dick
```

16

to become a griefer? Consider the MARINE
MERCENARY SQUAD. MMS will be selling our
services to whichever UE is the highest
bidder. DM me for details on tryouts.

—MMSRecruitment

griefsquad is here, as usual. reply to this
post with a poem about how you love drinking
the salty tears of the kings and you'll get an
invite

—teardrinker420

There were about a dozen more of the main factions, sprinkled in with hundreds of the usual assortment of desperates, who had no established faction in another server but who dreamed of building a successful, elite UE now there was a fresh start underway. I considered my options. I'd run with MMS before, on other servers, so I could probably skip the whole "tryouts." But with the server as new as it was, they might try to put me in charge of something…I decided to come back to them if I couldn't find anything better.

One post caught my eye: it wasn't an established faction, but neither did it seem like the typical desperate UE pipe dream.

Seeking five experienced, dedicated players
for a difficult and dangerous mission. HUGE
REWARDS. Details will be discussed in DMs.
Send brief resume. Faction (The Ocean Project)
will be dissolved following mission completion
or failure.

-Cubism

Now that was interesting. What kind of mission required only six players? Surely, any challenge would be easier with

17

more. And if the rewards were as "HUGE" as Cubism was claiming, wouldn't we want to transition this success into a Kingdom, rather than disband? Perhaps he was already pledged to one...

I checked The Ocean Project's faction page. Five members so far, Cubism and four others. There would only be one spot left. My curiosity far overpowered my doubts, however, and I abandoned the *PlanetCrash* tutorial to compose a suitably impressive introduction and résumé.

```
Cubism:

Your post in the LFG forum intrigues me. I'd
like to know more about The Ocean Project, and
especially the "huge rewards" it is supposed
to gain. My character on the NA-22 server is
Emily Everston. See below for my resume:

FPS/Marine main, specialty in orbital drop
missions.

Commanded a marine squad during the Battle of
Horizon, part of the only UE war thus far on
the NA-13 server. Ultimately victorious.

Served among the Marine Mercenary Squad on NA-
15, NA-16, and NA-20 servers. Veteran of 100+
active orbital drops on each of NA-15 and NA-
16, 25+ on NA-20. Recognized as "Marine of
Distinguished Skill" on NA-16 and NA-20.

Experience in other roles, including ship
command and crewing, mining, and
stealth/intelligence across other servers.
Playtime on NA-13 through NA-21 before today.
3000+ hours total. Check my player profile for
verification, I've given you viewing
permission.

-EDG2051
```

18

Cubism's response came a few minutes later, just as I was finishing the tutorial. I grinned: perfect timing.

```
Emily,

Nice resume. I think you'd be a good fit, a
marine specialist is the last thing I need for
my team. Welcome to the Ocean Project! Here's
the deal: I've found an exploit on the NA-22
server that will allow us to withdraw money
virtually from any bank used by a player to
pay for their NA-22 server access. Even if it
isn't ours. My best guess is that we can get
$50 million as a group this way. $8 million
for each of my team members, $10 million for
me, since I'm so damn clever and figured this
whole thing out.

I know you haven't agreed to anything yet, and
that this seems dubious. I can't force you,
but please, PLEASE, come to our first team
meeting before you talk about this with
anyone. ANYONE. Not your mother, your
girlfriend, or whoever else. If word of this
gets out, the devs could patch it out and the
opportunity will be lost. We'll also have to
move fast, before they can find it on their
own. Expect to put in a lot of hours.

The team will stay in touch via the chat room
linked here. We're having a meeting Saturday
at 5 PM GMT to discuss specifics and a plan of
action. Be there.

-Cubism
```

I was stunned. This couldn't possibly be real, could it? It had to be some sort of elaborate joke, a trick, a prank, something. But…eight million dollars? I couldn't even imagine what that would do for my life. I could drop out of school, never work a day in my life, and live comfortably forever, even if I reached a hundred and twenty years old. It was mind-boggling. For the second time, though, my curiosity overcame my doubts, and I set my phone alarm for noon on Saturday—since Boston was five hours behind GMT—and began working to build up my new character.

CHAPTER 5

One of the advantages of playing as a marine was that I could level up much more safely in the early game than other character types. As I ended the tutorial, I dropped onto NA-22's spawn planet, called Almanac. It was the only PvP-locked zone on the server, which meant that it was the only place you were safe from other players. Usually I, and most other players, wouldn't stick around here long, as there were better opportunities to get exp off-world, and the reset of death mattered a lot less when you had nothing. But in my case, I wanted to have a decent character for the first meeting, so risking death while trying to hit Level 2 wasn't going to be a good strategy. I'd be staying here for a while. I pulled up the default inventory as if I hadn't memorized it years back. Level 1 laser pulse rifle; five hundred energy credits; basic spacesuit; and a single ticket off-world, good for five light-years in any direction. There would usually be five-to-ten star systems in that range, far more than were that close to Earth IRL. Plus, the devs didn't bother to make systems that were completely useless, it was just a waste of energy. Every system had at least one useful planet, asteroid, or space-station.

The pulse rifle was a decent starting point. As a marine specialist, I'd be giving points to my Precision stat on levelling, alternating with Strength, while also putting one in Agility each level: at least for the first ten or so. I didn't need to waste time acquiring any specialist equipment before I knew what my specific role would be in Cubism's plan. So I headed straight to the PvP training arena. It was the only place on Almanac where PvP was unlocked, but even here you couldn't actually die, you simply respawned outside the entrance. You could challenge other players and the winner would get a small bit of exp. It wasn't the fastest way to level, but it was by far the safest. Unfortunately, falling behind in exp could be even worse than dying early. You'd end up behind everyone else, plus you get attached to your underpowered character. I was confident I'd do fine though. I was good enough.

I arrived at the PvP arena after about five minutes of travel and checked the current challenge postings. Since losing wouldn't hurt, I signed up for a fairly tough challenge: a two-on-one fight. To compound my exp winnings, I allowed the team I'd be facing to choose the map style and terrain. They made their selections and readied up.

The world went black as the match began.

Black faded to green and shapes began to emerge. A jungle terrain formed up around me, dense with trees and underscrub. I couldn't see where the enemy had spawned. They probably couldn't see me either.

"Commence match."

I hit the ground as soon as my character unfroze, already thankful for my extra point in Agility. The deep brush covered me entirely, rendering me near invisible. I crawled to the side. I didn't know if we'd been symmetrically spawned or not, but if we had it would give them a significant clue to my position. Laser blasts flew above me, searing the air. They cut across the jungle terrain, a random spray rather than an aimed blast. The enemy still had no idea where I was. I mentally marked where the blast had come from and pushed towards the location. The shooter had three options: he could stay put and hope I hadn't figured where the shots were coming from; he could run to a

22

new position (making a lot of noise in the process); or he could go to ground like I had and try to make his way through the underbrush. The third was the most dangerous for me, as it would put us on an even footing, which would benefit the duo over me on my own. That said, it was also the least likely. The PvP arena was generally occupied by newer players, yet unfamiliar with the game. They wouldn't be ready for the tactics of an experienced marine like me.

More blasts overhead. From another direction this time, which probably meant that it was his partner shooting. This confirmed that both of them were armed with the same Level 1 pulse rifles as I was. This was likely their first action in NA-22, same as me. Hopefully, this was their first action in *PlanetCrash* at all, seeking a two-on-one fight to get used to real combat.

I reoriented myself in the direction of the new blast. It was difficult to track an enemy based on a single laser blast, so I'd have to keep readjusting every time they fired, until they were in nearly opposite directions. For now they were both what I was calling "north," meaning forward from my starting position. You could get hopelessly lost in a place like this if you didn't keep a rigorous mental compass like I did. A lesson learned the hard way. The only way in *PlanetCrash*, sometimes.

A third blast, just ahead. I had a fix on one of the enemies. Careful not to make a sound, I pulled myself from my prone position and into a crouch, still keeping my head below the underscrub. I readied my weapon and then stood up. As I'd expected, one enemy was right in front of me, He turned in surprise, but I was already prepared. Three shots to the head should have been enough to put him down, but I fired a fourth to be safe. He went down after three, as expected, and the fourth raced off into the distance. All in one motion, I spun around and dove forward. The spin allowed me to confirm the location of the other target, at about ten o'clock from me. The dive was

23

to avoid his burst of fire in my direction, which followed almost instantly. I popped up again at my new position and treated him to four headshots of his own. Unfortunately, he was either clever or experienced. He too dove away immediately after firing, and only one of my shots connected.

I couldn't tell if it had been a headshot or not. He could be anywhere from 95% to 50% health, depending if he had any armor upgrades from his initial 500 EC, and on whether I'd scored a headshot. I remained upright as the target hit the ground again. Hopefully, I'd be able to get him as he rose to take a shot at me. A moment later, my opponent confirmed himself to be more clever than experienced: he fired at me from the ground. Not a bad idea in theory, but not something an experienced *PlanetCrash* player would ever do. He was about to learn why. Lasers were easily visible, so he'd confirmed his position to me, and had little time to shift it. I fired at the ground where he lay, a long, heavy burst, nearly pushing my rifle to overheat. A moment later the terrain faded.

"Match Complete." The robotic announcer confirmed my aim was true. 100 exp and 100 EC was the reward for winning. Not terrible for the five minutes I'd spent in the fight, but not nearly what I could have gotten in that amount of time off-world. Well, small risk meant small reward. They didn't call it "grinding" for nothing, though, so I began searching for my next matchup.

CHAPTER 6

Saturday came absurdly quickly and mind-numbingly slowly, both at the same time. Since showing up to a secret heist meeting as the least powerful team member seemed like bad form, I'd wanted time to build up my new character to a suitably impressive level. This was the origin of my sense that time was passing swiftly: I felt I should be bringing something better to the table than a Level 3 marine, but it was all I could get. On the other hand, this was the most exciting opportunity that had ever been put in front of me. My breathless impatience to know more gave Friday its glacial pace. I'd even reached the point of doing homework (on a *Friday*! My parents were thrilled) to distract myself from the waiting.

But, finally, *finally*, it came. At 11:56, four minutes before the meeting, I clicked the Discord link Cubism had sent. Better to be early than late. Most of the others had already joined, we were only missing two. Discord linked to *PlanetCrash* and would show our character names in the server. I did a quick once-over of the names of the three team members that had beaten me in. Publius Hadrianus was one. I recognized the name from Latin: it was that of a Roman Emperor. Jessica Nguyen and Valerie Peña were the others.

None of them were marked as the server admin, so I guessed Cubism himself hadn't arrived yet. I clicked to join the voice chat.

"Ayyyy, another one in!" Publius was the first to react to my entry. His voice was decently deep, probably an older teenage boy. But since he started his sentence with "ayyy" I doubted he was much older than I was.

"Hi Emily!" Valerie sounded a fair bit younger and managed to make even her two words bubble with energy. Some people had a problem with younger players, but I never thought it was too big a deal. They just had different strengths and weaknesses from the rest of us. I wouldn't put one in command, but I had no objections to having Valerie on the team. Hell, she'd probably have the fastest reaction time of any of us and might well end up saving all of our asses.

"Hey." That just left Jessica. Not much I could find out about her from just the one word, though.

"Hi everyone." I tried to sound friendly and keep the nerves out of my voice. Team chemistry is always key and seeming friendly always helps. I don't know if being friendly is even better. There are many things I can change about myself in *PlanetCrash*, but becoming an extrovert is not one of them. "What do you guys main? I'm a marine, myself."

"Sharpshooter!" Val replied. I grinned. It was the perfect role for a kid. No strategy, just skills. She'd be maxing her Precision stat to hit the most difficult shots our team would need to make, as opposed to the more balanced marine role.

As it turned out, Publius was on the opposite end of the skill/strategy spectrum: "I specialize in piloting, commanding, and managing mid-size ships. Frigates, mostly. That's probably as big as we can go anyway, given the size of the team."

It made sense to have someone like him on any good team. Sure, anyone could command a ship, but anyone could pick up a rifle as well. It helps to have specialists.

"Stealth and espionage," said Jessica. That was a relief, as I didn't like dying with a powered-down ship, as I had on NA-

21. At the same time, though, I had to stifle a laugh. The girl of few words and pure monotone seemed stereotypically ideal for the spymaster role.

Another player entered the server. It wasn't Cubism: there was no "Admin" role attached to his name, which was Jeremy O'Conor.

"What's up guys?"

I placed his accent immediately: he was from South Boston, a neighborhood only about five miles from where I lived. Only South Boston kids had that stereotypical Boston accent in this day and age.

"Heya, Jeremy!" I was the first to respond. "You from Southie?"

"Damn right I am! What about you?"

"JP," I replied. It was the nickname of my neighborhood, Jamaica Plain. "What's your main?"

We took a few minutes to rehash our previous conversation for Jeremy's benefit. He didn't have a main character build at all, as it turned out. He was what we called a "flex" player, a sort of jack-of-all trades, master of none. I guessed he'd be the understudy for a specific role if any of us dropped suddenly or failed to show up for a mission. He could also assist in dozens of ways when all of us were present.

Overall, I was impressed with the team. Cubism seemed like he'd done a good job putting us together.

Once the discussions of role were finished, we turned to small talk as we waited for Cubism to join the server and begin the meeting, where we'd finally find out what crazy plan he'd cooked up to make us all millionaires.

CHAPTER 7

"Hello everyone. I'm Cubism; my character name for NA-Twenty-Two is Jesse Lee. You've all been briefed on the general situation, but I'd like to take a moment to fill in the specifics. There are two security flaws in *PlanetCrash*'s latest server that we're going to exploit. First, there's an inventory issue that allows us to insert and execute unintended code on the game server. With the right collection of items, we can convince the game that it's no longer looking at a list of items in an inventory, but rather as code that needs to be executed. The items we need range in rarity from common to legendary. This is the primary reason I needed a good team: I can't get them myself. Secondly, *PlanetCrash* stores the banking information of everyone who paid to get on the server. You all gave your information to get on here, as did I, as did seven hundred fifty thousand others. We will use the inventory exploit to transfer all the money in every account connected to this server to ourselves."

There was a moment of silence.

"So we're just...taking thousands of people's life savings?" I asked.

"Oh, no, of course not," Cubism replied, seeming ready for the question. "The FDIC insures all deposits in the US. And the FDIC gets its funding from member banks, so at the end of the day we're just taking a couple bucks out of the pockets of the megabanks. I don't think I'll be losing any sleep over that, do you?"

Now that I was fine with. Mergers and acquisitions over the past few decades had left only about a dozen banks in the world and they were all massive, making trillions of dollars. The millions we'd be lifting would barely even be missed.

"Publius here. But it is against the law, right? If we get caught after the heist, if they trace the money or something, it will mean prison?"

"Good question," Cubism replied. "In fact, it's not entirely clear what law is being broken. Video game hacking is very much the 'wild west' of criminal law, with little established precedent. A smart lawyer could maybe get us off. But in any case, I'm going to convert the money to Shadowcoin and pay you that way. We'll lose about fifteen percent in value but then it's untraceable."

Shadowcoin was a popular crypto-currency from Estonia, one that was fast becoming the world's most popular alternative to traditional currencies.

Jeremy had the next question. "Do you have the list of items we need? Can you distribute that?"

"Absolutely. I'll send it around now." A notification popped up on my HUD, showing a new message from "Jesse Lee." I pulled it up immediately. Wow…when Cubism had said that the items in question "ranged" in rarity from common to legendary, I'd thought it'd be a little more balanced towards common, as average items are. But twenty-three of the fifty items were legendary, the highest rarity in the game. Every item was assigned one of four "rarities": common; rare; epic; and legendary. Usually, having one or two legendaries was an accomplishment, but we were going to need twenty-three between us. Almost four each: this was going to take some doing. No wonder he'd needed a solid team.

"How do we start?" Valerie asked.

29

"Have you discussed your roles with each other yet?" Cubism verified we had before continuing. "Jessica will put her information skills to good use, looking for leads on the items we need. Once she finds something, Publius will fly us in and Emily will lead a few of us as a strike team to extract. Once we have all the items, I'll activate the bug, and you'll all get your millions in Shadowcoin. In the meantime, though, while you're waiting for Jessica, just focus on building up your character. We're going to need a tough squad."

My breath caught. *They're relying on me to lead FPS fights?* I should have expected it: it was how I'd presented myself on my resumé that I'd given to Cubism. And yes, I'd been squad leader in extraction missions before, but that didn't mean I was *good* at it. Well, so be it. I was the only one on the team qualified to command an FPS squad. If becoming a multimillionaire required me to lead a few raids, I could lead a few raids. *But if these turned out like the last time I tried...*I pushed the negative thought out of my head. It wasn't a productive way to go about my life, always stuck on the NA-13 server and the mistakes of the past.

"How do we know all of this will even work?" Jeremy asked.

"I'm glad you asked," Cubism said. "Let me transfer you some items." A moment passed in silence.

"Got them. Wow, okay, I'm convinced."

"What happened?" I asked.

"See for yourself." A moment later, a notification came up in *PlanetCrash* that Jeremy's character was trying to transfer me some items. I accepted the transfer and opened my inventory. An eclectic assortment of common items had been added to my inventory.

"Sort them by the custom labeling," Cubism said, "Jeremy probably sent them to you alphabetically."

30

So he had. It was the default, after all. As soon as I resorted into Cubism's customer order, an option popped up on my screen to change my character's name. That wasn't supposed to be possible: names were supposed to be fixed from character creation until death.

"That's about the most interesting thing it's possible to do with common items," Cubism said, almost apologetically. I took his word for it, and transferred the items onto Val.

"Everyone clear?" He asked, once we'd all seen the effects. Each of us grunted an affirmation to Cubism's question. "Then let's break. Get out there and level up those characters. You'll need them to be the best in the server."

CHAPTER 8

Shortly after the meeting ended, I received a direct message from Jeremy.

```
hey emily. i was thinking we should level
together for a bit, get a feel for each others
playstyles. were the two top marines in the
group, it'll be good if were on the same
wavelength
```

It was a good idea. Honestly, if Cubism was expecting me to lead everyone in battles, I should probably have a one-on-one farm session with each of them individually.

```
Absolutely. You free now?
```

I booted the game after sending my reply. His affirmative came in the form of a private voice call request, which I answered immediately. "Hello again!"

"Hey," he responded. "Gimme a second, I'm launching the game now."

"Yeah, no problem." I took the time to review my in-game settings for the thousandth time. Mouse sensitivity, resolution, graphics settings: all exactly as I liked them. They never changed; the check was more a ritual than an actual necessity for me.

"Aright, I'm in. What was your in-game name again?"

"Emily Everton. ID number is one, one, eight, three, two: in case there's someone else with the name."

"Nope, just you. Okay, friend request is in."

I accepted his request and pulled up his profile. Jeremy was a little ahead of me, holding an exp advantage of just over a level. It looked like he'd gotten a cash windfall as well; his pulse rifle had been upgraded with an improved heatsink. He'd be able to fire more times than I could before resetting or risking overheat. That said, it didn't matter much how many shots you had. What you did with them was far more important. Time to see what he was made of.

I invited him to my party. "Where do you want to go?"

"I don't think the bossman will much appreciate if two of his team go off and die together immediately after that pitch," Jeremy responded wryly. "Let's try something safe."

"Fair enough. PvE on Almanac?"

Almanac was where I'd been levelling the whole weekend and I was less than excited to go back. I had suggested PvE as a break from the endless duels I'd ground out before. Jeremy sighed audibly enough for me to hear over his microphone. It seemed he was no more thrilled about Almanac than I.

Usually the first levels of *PlanetCrash* were the most exciting. Seeking out whatever unique planets existed on the server, battling against horrors with crappy gear…and very little to lose if you screwed up. Almanac was the exact opposite of that, a planet that existed in exactly the same way on every server: a safe haven for people who thought they had something to lose even at low level. In our case, we actually did, so Almanac, while boring, became useful.

"Okay," Jeremy said a moment later. "Let's get going."

A significant advantage of Almanac was that you could teleport there as long as there were no hostiles nearby, so we saved some travel time as well.

33

Our first joint mission was trivial enough to allow for small talk alongside our tactical communication.

It turned out that Jeremy was seventeen, only a year older than I was, and had dropped out of high school on his birthday, the first day it was legally allowed.

"There was an 'exit interview,'" he told me. "Legally required. They sit you down in a room with all your teachers and the principal, then they shame you for a bit, tell you how great and wicked important education is and how you'll regret dropping out. I don't, by the way, so they can suck it."

"Do they make you justify why you're leaving?" I asked.

"I mean, they ask, and if you don't have a reason they consider *valid* or whatever, there's more shame coming your way after. All a bunch of stupid crap. School would have just stood in the way of our little heist, anyway, though I didn't know that when I quit."

"So...are you working on the side? Or just full-time in *PlanetCrash*?"

"Don't have a job at the moment. Got an interview tomorrow, maintaining construction bots. Don't know that I'll take it, even if I get the offer. Damn things cost my dad his job. And his life. Working on them seems like it might be an insult. Or maybe it keeps the family in construction. I don't know, honestly."

Over the past decades, construction had become almost entirely automated, performed by yellow construction bots. Humans couldn't compete with bots that were faster, more precise, and who never needed to be paid. Thousands of jobs had been lost. It had caused a major political shakeup. These days, the only humans in construction were the architects and the bot maintenance guys, who kept all of the construction bots in good order. I guessed the maintenance would be automated eventually, as well.

34

"I'm sorry for your loss." I didn't know what else to say.

"Don't be. Not like he was a good person anyway." Jeremy was trying his best to sound callous and strong, but underneath I could hear the pain in his voice. It was probably best just to let this drop for now. We finished up the remainder of our warm-up mission with a tense silence between us. When it did end, though, I decided to break the silence with something mundane. Something in-game, rather than in the world it seemed Jeremy was desperate to escape.

"That went smoothly,' I said after a victorious battle. "Do we want to kick up the difficulty by a few notches?"

"Yeah." He chuckled. "I want to see how you do in a *real* fight, Emily. Need to know if I can trust my financial future to your hands." The comment was teasing, playful. It seemed his tension had evaporated a while ago. Relief flooded into me. Heavy conversations like that were never my speciality.

"Oh, I'll be fine," I replied, attempting to artificially match his air of confidence. "So long as you don't drag me down." He gave a little gasp, mockingly, pretending like he'd been grievously insulted.

I began scrolling through the list of available PvE missions in our vicinity, filtering them to a difficulty at our current level rather than below it, as we'd started with. One caught my eye: it was flagged as a "unique mission," so the first player or team to complete it would get a randomized extra reward beyond what you'd normally expect from a mission of that difficulty. Missions like this would appear occasionally with no warning, then disappear again as soon as someone beat them. Really, the only way to get one was to be staring at the PvE missions list when it showed up. Which, conveniently, I had been.

"A unique mission just popped at our level. Two miles southwest. Let's get moving." I didn't wait for Jeremy to confirm, nor did he pause for any further details. We both knew the

35

importance of every second in ensuring none of the thousands of other players on the server would beat us to the finish line. It was comforting to play with someone who was on the same wavelength as I was. So often I'd done something like this, only to start walking off without my companion and having to turn around, explain, and waste valuable time.

"Brief me," Jeremy said as we walked. "What's the mission?"

"It's a cool one. A hostage situation. The story is that a civil servant has been captured and is now being held by a group rebelling against the government of Almanac. No player-controlled factions are involved, by the way, just the Almanac government and the rebels. We'll be the only players in there. The catch is that we have to extract the target from the cave where they're holding him *unharmed.* So we'll have to be fast and really careful with our shots. No stray plasma blasts on this one."

"Does unharmed mean alive or uninjured?" Jeremy asked.

"Not permanently injured. If he bruises his shin that's fine. If he gets shot that's not."

"Got it."

"Okay, we're close enough to the mission to launch it whenever we're ready. You good to go?"

"Absolutely. Let's do it."

I triggered the mission.

The environment changed subtly as I loaded in. The skies became overcast rather than the sunny blue they'd been before and the trees seemed to darken as well. The game was setting a rather gloomy mood and it was easy to get lost in that. I shivered involuntarily, my brain sensing a temperature drop in *PlanetCrash*, even though no change had occurred at my computer.

36

Visibility was low, but we knew from the mission parameters where the cave should be located within the area. Movement became its own challenge now. We were still on the clock, trying to be the first to complete the quest, but stealth was also a factor. If we sprinted in the direction of the cave, as we'd been doing until I'd formally launched the mission, we'd be detected by hostiles and picked off from afar. Finding the right balance of speed and stealth was tricky and tense. Were we going too slow, letting another team overtake us? Or were we going too loud, with snipers lining up shots on us?

"Eyes on target," Jeremy whispered. "Three o'clock."

"Got it." I kept my voice low as well. Rationally I knew it didn't matter, our voices weren't even transmitted to the game, but you could never shake the feeling that the world of *Planet-Crash* was real.

The cave was unimpressive, appearing to be little more than a hole in a boulder on another of the endless forested hills of this part of Almanac.

"Let's sweep the area outside, check for guards. You okay to take point?" I asked.

"Roger."

I followed Jeremy as he pushed straight up the hill. It was a bold, perhaps risky move, taking the high ground. It would give us a good vantage to look for guards, but simultaneously make us easier to spot. It largely depended on whether the tree coverage was dense or sparse on the far side of the hill. I didn't argue the point. It was a valid tactic and I wanted to see how he'd behave without my influence.

We stopped at the top of the hill and crouched down, trying to minimize our profile. I checked behind us to ensure we weren't being outflanked when Jeremy spoke. "There's a patrol at the base of the hill. Two guards, armed. Let's take 'em down quietly."

My heart sped up. "Got it," I replied, glad my voice sounded calm in my ears. I tried never to betray my emotions in combat. "Lead the way."

We started down the hill, not directly across the way we had come up, but at an angle to the side. I was pleased when I spotted the patrol, noticing that Jeremy wasn't leading us directly towards them, but with an approach that meant when we reached the base of the hill we'd be a little ways behind them.

Now that we knew where the enemy was, it was easier to maintain stealth. We darted from tree to tree, using the brush as cover for our movements. I'd equipped forest camouflage armor before the mission, so I was next to invisible. Jeremy had neglected to: he was still wearing jet black. It was intimidating, to be sure, but we weren't trying to scare these guards. I felt a twinge of annoyance at him, but he spoke before I could point this out.

"There's a boulder up ahead. Should make for a good ambush spot. Let's head over."

My irritation disappeared as my brain shifted into high gear, preparing for the fight. There was a small drip of adrenaline in my veins in anticipation, though it was utterly negligible compared to the flood I knew was coming.

We pressed up against the boulder for a few moments before the voices of the patrol came into earshot. They were just NPCs, non-player characters generated by the game solely for this mission, but their discussion demonstrated the care that PlanetCrash Studios put into this game. We might be the only ones ever to hear this discussion about how one of the guard's marriage was suffering. Well, I was about to make it worse.

"I'll take the left one out, you take the right. On my signal." I took over leadership, as I wasn't sure what trigger Jeremy was waiting for to begin the ambush.

"Affirmative," he responded.

"Go." I gave the command as they came into a range where they might see us.

Jeremy simply raised his weapon and fired twice; I took a step away from the boulder to ensure he wasn't in my firing line before downing the second guard. Both guards took two shots in the head to kill, just as expected.

"Let's check the bodies," Jeremy suggested.

"No. Someone else might have heard the shots. We're doubly on the clock if they're reinforcing. Head towards the cave. I'll take point."

He fell in behind me without a complaint as I moved to the cave entrance.

"Want me to flash in?" Jeremy asked.

"You've got flashbangs already?" I was fairly surprised. Flashbang grenades—any grenades, really—were generally hard to get in *PlanetCrash*. In the confined halls of a spacecraft, they could easily turn the tide of a fight, making them invaluable for boarding parties. Their price was consistently high, both because of pirate types who wanted to hijack ships and the UEs remaining mobilized for war.

"Yeah," he replied. "Ten. Lucky loot drop for my grind over the last week."

In theory, a flashbang would be equally valuable in a cave, but I didn't think it worth using for this mission.

"Save it. We might be boarding ships at some point for this project. I'll breach and check right side."

I took a few deep breaths, then stepped inside the cave. I swung immediately to my right, checking the ninety-degree area from twelve o'clock to three o'clock, which hadn't been visible from outside. It was clear. Behind me, Jeremy fired two shots.

"Clear left," he said.

39

"Clear right."

I took a moment to examine the inside of the cave, no longer singularly focused on the immediate breach. We seemed to be in a large, artificial underground room rather than a natural cave. There was a decent amount of cover in the event of a firefight, pillars, mainly, for structural support. Three hallways extended into the dark, each going deeper underground.

A light flickered at the back of one of the tunnels and my adrenaline began to pump.

"Get in cover!" A flickering light wasn't much to go on, but I had a bad feeling about this. I dove behind one of the pillars and took aim at the tunnel entrance. Out of the corner of my eye, I saw Jeremy follow suit. The light became solid, then brightened. A rocket flew out of the tunnel, impacting and exploding just behind us. I was thrown to the ground by the pressure wave from the explosion and my shields were largely shredded. Dust and debris from the explosion hung in the air, and my HUD registered toxicity in the air, another timer on this mission.

Troops began to flood in from the other two tunnels. I crawled back behind the pillar I'd been using as cover, hoping to get a moment's reprieve to recharge my shield. No such luck, however. The enemy opened fire and their rifles chipped away at the stone pillar. It wouldn't last long in these conditions.

Jeremy's return fire began almost instantly. In the chaos of the explosion, I hadn't seen what happened to him, but it seemed like I'd taken the brunt of the damage. Popping a few shots blindly around the left side of the pillar, I then sprinted away to the right. Another, thicker pillar stood only a few feet away, which would make for more substantial cover.

En route, I took a few hits, removing the rest of my shielding, but not enough to pierce my body armor, and no headshots, so I stood strong. My habit of taking points in Agility was paying off already: I'd have been exposed a lot longer if I hadn't been focusing it. Reaching the pillar, I went back to blind fire.

This was one of the few advantages of facing massed troops as a duo and the only tactic that made it viable. Each of their soldiers had to take careful aim to have any chance of hitting us, and cover could shield us from the majority of their fire as long as we managed to prevent them from flanking us. At the same time, I could stick my gun around the pillar and shoot in their vague direction, using my kill feed for confirmation that Jeremy and I were hitting targets.

This reflection reminded me to check for flankers and, indeed, a squad of five was trying to push around my left side. This time precision would be necessary. I took more careful aim before dropping two of them with shots to the head. The other three split apart and went for cover, their flanking attempt broken.

When I returned to checking the main pack, I found that they'd largely gone to cover as well. We'd thinned out their ranks enough that there was sufficient cover for all of them. Probably there were about ten to twenty left.

"I'll bait," I said to Jeremy. Baiting was a well-known tactic within *PlanetCrash* for dealing with computer-controlled units who outnumbered you and were in cover. You had one player expose themselves to shoot at something. It didn't matter what. One or two of the AI enemies would reveal themselves to try to return your fire and your buddy would headshot them to take them out. There was no doubt in my mind that Jeremy would have done this a thousand times.

As I'd expected, as soon as I left cover, Jeremy lit up my kill feed with two more soldiers. It was faster than I'd hoped; Jeremy was excellent with his rifle.

We repeated this process, alternating who was the bait and who was the trap until they stopped taking the bait. This could have meant that we'd killed them all, but that wasn't necessarily the case. There was a chance that the last few were simply waiting for us to relax our guard.

"Let's clear this out. I'll stay right side." I gave the order and moved out of my cover, rifle raised. No response so far. Pushing up against the far right wall, I circled around until I could see behind the pillars that they'd been using as cover. Jeremy did the same from the opposite wall.

Nothing but bodies remained.

"I think we're clear."

"We're lucky the target wasn't in here," Jeremy said, humor in his voice. "We totally forgot about careful shooting for a while."

I chuckled, the energizing relief of another combat victory flowing through me. "I don't know that we could have survived the beginning of that by picking targets carefully."

"Fair enough." He paused for a moment. "Which tunnel do you want to explore first? Rocket, army, or the third one?"

"Let's try the third one. I'd rather not run into any more rockets or armies."

"I feel that. Let's move."

He took the lead again. In an enclosed space like the tunnel, he was taking a role known in *PlanetCrash* as the "entry-fragger." It was a bit of a misnomer, as the entry-fragger wasn't supposed to get the majority of the "frags," which was slang for kills. The job was to draw attention and fire to himself and be the sole focus of any hostiles. Usually the entry-fragger would shoot a bit wildly, hoping to get a lucky hit. In our hostage scenario, though, Jeremy would hold his fire entirely. As I was backing him up, it was my job to take careful aim and secure kills. Tactics like this were common for squads of up to about five soldiers, with a couple additional roles for the people in the

42

back, the "supports." For now, though, it was just the two of us.

Jeremy pushed open the first door we encountered, throwing himself clear of the doorway to give me unobstructed aim. I leaned around the corner with my rifle up, my aim snapping onto the first head I saw. A split second of hesitation was enough for me to confirm that this was not the hostage, and I took the shot. As my target fell, I looked up from my weapon to get a wide view of the room. Two more hostiles, no hostage. I took them down with a few more well-placed shots. Jeremy was hiding behind a table as the last enemy fell. He'd recognized, like I had, that the hostage wasn't in the room, and had taken advantage of that to blind fire, keeping the attention on him for the few extra moments that I'd needed to clear the room.

The door on the far side of the room flew open before we'd had a chance to move and a squad moved in. They were using a human shield; they'd brought the hostage right to us. Thoughtful of them. The problem with human shields is this: either you expose your head from behind the hostage, or you can't see. In this particular case, they'd elected to see: a fatal mistake against sharpshooters as precise as Jeremy and I were. We simultaneously put shots into the head of the guy holding the hostage. A few seconds later, the other four hostiles lay in heaps on the ground. The hostage blinked, shocked but unharmed.

Jeremy took the lead on interacting with him. "You doing okay, sir?"

The hostage nodded. I noted that Jeremy had defaulted into a respectful tone with the NPC, who wouldn't even be able to appreciate it.

"I'll check the back room, first," I chipped in. "Cover the front." Jeremy moved into position and raised his rifle, peeking around the door.

I stepped into the back room. It was an obvious loot room, with a large chest sitting in the center of the room and no other furnishing. Given that reinforcements could come at any moment, I looted the entire inventory of the chest without bothering to check what it was.

"Okay, let's get you out of here," I said to the hostage as I returned. I turned to Jeremy. "You watch the front, I'll take behind. Move out."

We made it out of the cave without event. Upon exiting, the hostage vanished into a small explosion of fireworks. That was the signal: we were the first to finish the mission. We'd get to keep the rewards. Exp and EC poured into my account, enough to level me up twice. I continued to pour my stats into Agility, wanting to push it a quite a bit higher before taking too much in the other categories. It was the only stat, save for Manufacturing, that skill couldn't compensate for.

I checked my inventory to see what I'd looted. A couple of small but valuable grenades, plus an automatic plasma shotgun. It was a weapon of massive damage, large spread (save for when wielded by players with the highest precision stats), and wanton ruination.

The irony made me laugh. We'd just completed a mission where we'd been focusing so hard on making each shot accurate, yet the reward was the most random weapon I'd ever seen. This would have been utterly unusable for the latter part of the hostage rescue we'd just done: we would have accidentally shot the target a dozen times over.

I showed it to Jeremy. "You want this?" I asked.

44

"Nah," he responded. "I've already got some nice gear; you've gotta catch up somehow." It seemed his teasing never turned off.

"Thanks." I equipped the shotgun in my secondary slot, leaving my preferred pulse rifle as my primary weapon. The pulse rifle was statistically weaker than the shotgun; it did lower damage per second, or DPS as we called it. But statistics weren't everything. It didn't matter how much DPS you weapon had if you never hit anything, so it was always a good idea to keep your comfort weapons close. I was familiar with plasma shotguns, of course, but only used them situationally. They weren't my go to and probably never would be.

"That's about all I've got time for," Jeremy said. He hesitated. "I think we'll work well together. Really. I've got high hopes for this project."

I was caught off-guard by the sincerity of the statement. "Yeah. I...uh. Same. I think this will work out."

"Catch you later." He abruptly disconnected from Discord in the awkward silence that followed, and I followed him out.

CHAPTER 9

School on Monday was worse than usual. Slower. Time impeded with the knowledge that each minute was a minute spent falling behind the rest of the team. Except, perhaps, Val, who was young enough that she'd likely be in school as well.

"Care to rejoin us, Emily?" Mr Adams jarred me back into Algebra 2 and out of *PlanetCrash*. It wasn't said in an unkind way; it wasn't a callout. But he, like all of my teachers, knew that I was struggling a bit and, unlike some of my teachers, legitimately cared about my performance. It didn't help; it only made me feel worse about being a poor student.

I looked up and nodded at Mr. Adams.

"Thank you," he responded, before launching back into an explanation of polynomial factorization. It was gibberish to me and I tuned it out almost immediately. One refocus from Mr Adams in one class was not going to outdo an entire year of in-attention. He started to walk around the classroom. Handing something back? He got to my desk and slid a piece of paper onto it dispassionately. Mr Adams didn't meet my eye, which meant I'd done badly. Not liking to see students fail, he found it hard to give out poor grades, like the one I'd inevitably gotten on this quiz.

I flipped it over. *Ah, crap.* Seventeen percent was a new low for me. I'd have to get this signed, have to show it to my parents and get hit with another lecture. Great. Or I could just forge dad's signature again. I was getting pretty good at it anyway.

That meant the end of class, though, so I could soon shuffle off into my free period. True to my prediction, the bell rang just as Mr Adams handed back the last of the quizzes. The man had an impeccable sense of timing.

My classmates and I had been mentally preparing for this and we surged up and towards the door as one. Leaving class for my free was always a great weight off my shoulders. It was the same for most people, I guessed, but for different reasons. For my classmates, it was a break from the draining and stressful race for grades we were put through. For me, I wasn't even in the race. The free was a break from knowing that I should be doing something else.

With my poor performance, though, I was required to spend my "free periods" in the school's small library. The idea was that we'd spend that time studying and getting ahead on homework, offsetting our poor performance. Well, you can take a horse to water, but you can't make me drink. I spent many of my free periods making plans for the evening's *PlanetCrash* session. Where to go, how to maximize my exp gain...

My phone vibrated. We mere "low achieving" students weren't supposed to check it during our fake frees, but I wasn't about to let that stop me.

My breath caught. It was a message from Cubism.

```
Team,

Jessica has located the first of the rare
items. This one is in an easy enough spot that
we should be able to get it with our current
characters, but we have to leave soon. Mission
is going to launch in 5 minutes. Get here
fast.

Cubism
```

47

I was torn. I'd have to ditch not only the school's library, but the entire school building, since the nearest *PlanetCrash* access was at the Boston Public Library, two blocks away. For a student in my position, that'd be considered truancy. The administration thought many things about me, but mostly they were sympathetic. This might well ruin that...

To hell with the administration. Millionaires didn't need high school diplomas, now, did they?

I quietly gathered my things into my backpack, careful not to draw attention. As soon as I was set, I bolted for the door, away to freedom, to *PlanetCrash*.

CHAPTER 10

I accelerated once I'd crashed through the door and onto the street. It was the perfect time: after the morning bustle of commuters had ended but before people started heading to lunch on Newbury street. With no crowds in my way, I blew through the streets to the library. Ordinarily a five-minute walk, I arrived in less than two. Once inside the building, among the high, vaulted ceilings and shelves upon shelves of books, I slowed down. A powerwalk carried me up the stairs and toward the "teens" section of the library. It was a dedicated set of three rooms; the entry room was densely packed with bookshelves, much like the areas outside, but with higher shelf density, to fit a carefully catered selection of the library's YA books.

On the right of that main room of the teen section was the graphic novel and comic section. It wasn't a room in which I spent much of my time. That dubious honor fell to the third room, the room to the far left, the room I was headed towards now. It was a lounge and gaming section: a thousand square feet of comfy chairs to read the novels and comics from the other rooms, of PCs (beefy enough to run *PlanetCrash*, which was no mean feat, even ten years after its original release), and of tables to play board games on. Adults weren't permitted in the section without a chaperone who was thirteen to nineteen years old. I loved the place. I had never slept there, but it felt more like home than anywhere else outside of *PlanetCrash*.

I slid into the chair behind my favorite of the PCs and started the *PlanetCrash* install. While it was still tough to run the game at decent framerates, the install had drastically decreased in time to download. This was thanks largely to Boston's effort to provide free internet access universally throughout the city. The competition had finally gotten the old internet service providers off their butts to upgrade their networks and improve connection speeds. It was the only way to compete with "free." The library had invested some of its funding into the privatized, higher-speed internet access, for which I was eternally grateful. It cut the *PlanetCrash* download to just about five minutes. So less than ten minutes after ditching study hall, I had launched *PlanetCrash*, logged in, and connected to Discord.

The others had already assembled, save for Valerie, who, the others informed me, was unable to cut out of class as easily as we were.

"What's the situation?"

"PvE location," Jessica said. "Planet is called Orisa-B. Item drop that will be there is the *Armor of Vulnerability*."

"Plot a course for Orisa-B," Cubism instructed Publius, who was already at the helm.

"Aye aye."

Jessica continued unfazed. "It's kind of a useless item outside of our plans, so I doubt we'll run into any opposition."

"Useless?" Jeremy asked.

I spoke up, already familiar with the item. "Whenever you put it on, you get resistance to one chosen type of damage but weakness to two random others. Not too helpful unless there's only going to be one type of attack in a fight."

Jessica nodded. "It's not exactly a great find, for a rare item." She pulled up a map of the planet in question on the vidscreen. "It's somewhere in this sector here. Enemies around

50

should be anti-human robots, mostly about level eight. A little higher than us, but a good source of exp if we can pull it off."

I pointed to an area of the map. "We should drop here, take the high ground. The AHRs will hate us landing in their territory, so we're going to need to get entrenched quickly up there. Probably all enemies in a two-klick radius will push onto our position. Once that assault ends, we can sweep across the area much more easily. Jeremy, equip a sniper rifle or DMR if you have one. Val's not here, so we're relying on you for longer range fire support."

"Seems risky, letting them attack us like that," Publius called back from the helm.

"They're going to converge on us no matter what," I replied. "We either do it as a stealth mission and try never to get detected, or we fight from an entrenched position. If we do stealth, we're passing up on the exp. Plus if we run into them unexpectedly we'll be as good as dead. There's no way to eliminate the risk."

Cubism nodded and calibrated the drop pods for the hill I'd specified. "How far out are we?" He asked Publius.

"About three minutes."

"Suit up everyone. Stand by for planetcrash."

Planetcrash was the titular mechanic of the game and what had attracted so many players to have a go when it launched. There had been space combat games before, with battles between capital ships and fighters, and there had been MMOFPS before, dozens upon dozens of each. *PlanetCrash* was the first game to successfully and seamlessly combine the two. Players could be fired out of orbital ships and onto planets to fight a land war. It added tactical and strategic depth to both the space and land combat, it connected both playstyles into a single experience, and, most importantly, it was the most exhilarating

51

experience in the world. It was the core of the reason why I continually chose to be a marine on server after server.

Suiting up didn't take long. As per my suggested strategy, I equipped my heaviest armor for the drop: defense would be far more important than mobility in the upcoming battle. I was still using the standard-issue pulse rifle that all players began their characters with, but I'd spent some of my EC to upgrade it up to 6 to match my character. The loot I'd found so far had failed to provide anything powerful enough to make it worth dropping, save for the plasma shotgun that was my secondary.

"One minute out. Into the pods."

I stepped into the drop pod nearest me. Publius could fire these out of the ship at extreme speeds, landing us on the planet's surface in seconds. Another miracle of a better world that wasn't possible IRL. The pod sealed behind me. Nothing to do now but wait.

"Thirty seconds."

I tried to slow my breathing, calm my nerves. It only vaguely helped.

"Ten seconds to planetcrash…five seconds…go!"

The pod exploded from our team's frigate, hitting the Orisa-B atmosphere before I had time to react. Re-entry was a chaotic cacophony of intense vibration, blinding light, and the roar of the wind. Logically, I knew that the pod wouldn't burn up, and that even if it did I was safe in the library, but no amount of logic could overwhelm the sheer *feeling* of danger planetcrash could give.

My pod burst through the turbulence of re-entry and into the atmosphere. I hurtled towards the landing hill, streaking across the skies of Orisa-B.

Impact.

I burst out of the pod, pulse rifle already leveled. Almost instantly, laser blasts were streaking all around me from the robotic forces. *Crap!* I hadn't expected them to reach us nearly this quickly. We'd have no time to set up defenses. I aimed quickly, taking down three assailants with a blast from my rifle. Shots came from behind me as well; we were surrounded already. A second pod hit the ground just a few meters from mine. That would be Jeremy: as the best marines on the team, Publius would have dropped us first.

"We're already surrounded; use your pods as cover." We would go down quickly if everyone else burst out of their pods as aggressively as I had. Jeremy reacted to the update instantly. His pod door opened just a sliver, and he began firing out of it. The other two pods, carrying Jessica and Cubism, smashed down as well, their occupants staying inside. They'd be safe inside, for a time at least, but we'd be overrun eventually.

An idea struck me.

"Publius, how much fuel left in the pods?"

A pause as he checked. "Only a little in each. Not enough for an extraction. Why?"

"Can you get them rearranged into a circle?"

"I think so. Hold on everyone." The pods blasted off the ground, singeing me and taking most of my health. I dove into the crater mine had left behind for momentary cover. A second later, they crashed back down again, each on their side, forming a circle around me. Publius even managed to land them with their doors facing inward, allowing the team to disembark.

I dug myself out of the crater and clambered atop on the of the pods as the others collected in the circle.

"I've got the north side covered," I called out as I rested my rifle in the gap between two of the pods for stability. "Jeremy, take south; Cubism east, and Jessica west." They hustled into their positions. I'd placed Jeremy directly behind me be-

53

cause I trusted his skill the most. It would be easy enough to check on the others and ensure they weren't getting overrun. Another burst from my rifle felled another small group of androids, another drop evaporated from the tide that threatened to crush us.

I had to time my bursts carefully to maximize my effectiveness: too short, and I would be wasting time, but too long and my rifle would overheat. After a few minutes, however, I had this deadly rhythm down to muscle memory, allowing me to check in on my squadmates. Cubism was holding his own and there was a solid five meters between him and the nearest enemy. Jessica wasn't quite as strong, the robots were making incremental gains against her position. Whether she could hold alone depended largely on how many reinforcements would descend upon us.

I spun my rifle to take down three of the androids getting overly close to her, before turning back towards my own horde. Even my momentary distraction had allowed them to advance on me, so I refocused my efforts, working to make each shot count.

I froze momentarily, realizing that I'd been neglecting to check my shield strength. *Stupid!* Just because it wasn't on my primary HUD didn't mean it wasn't important. I pulled up the panel. Only seventeen percent shield strength left. The others hadn't been on the ground as long, so they'd probably have more juice left. Couldn't hurt to check though.

"Shield check everyone! I'm at seventeen percent!"

"Twenty-one." Cubism's reply was immediate.

"Twenty-five."

"Thirty-two," Jeremy chimed in. "You can be in awe of my skills whenever you want."

I smiled, my spirits lifted both by Jeremy's banter and by the decent shield strength left on each of my allies.

54

"Publius, when I hit five percent, can you dive-bomb this position? It'll pull fire off of us, give us a chance to recharge our shields."

"Roger that; readying weapons now."

I kept my shield HUD up for the next few minutes, keeping one eye on the android army and the other on my rapidly dwindling shield strength. Twelve percent, then eleven, then ten. Another burst from my rifle laid waste to the newest front-line of enemy troops.

My shield status went red in my vision: I'd fallen below three percent shield while I wasn't looking. Another sloppy mistake...I was severely out of practice at being in charge of a marine squad.

"Publius, now!" I called. "Everyone else, down and re-charge."

Hiding behind the pods for a few moments would allow us the downtime to get our shield strength back, but would leave the robots unchecked. I ducked down and after a moment my shields started to tick back up.

The frigate came screaming down from the outer atmosphere, all its guns blazing with a brilliant light. Explosions echoed on all sides, and the dirt they threw up rained down from above, dusting each of us. Publius came around for another pass and once again we were amidst a chaotic field of debris.

"I gotta pull out," Publius said after a few more passes. "They'll be ready for another one and I might not make it out."

His run had lasted a few minutes in total. I checked my shields. Seventy percent.

"You're good, get out of here!" I replied, and retook my position atop the wall of pods. The frigate attack run had gathered some extra space between us and the enemy, so some of the pressure was off from that as well.

The battle dragged on in much the same way for hours. Someone's shield would get low, Publius would drop in to give us a minute to recharge, and we'd retake our positions somewhat refreshed. As the local sun, Orisa, fell onto the horizon, the oncoming ranks began to thin, and by twilight the battle was ours. Jeremy and I had managed to collect enough exp to level up twice; Cubism and Jessica once. Overall, a resounding success, despite my blunders towards the beginning.

We caught our breath while Publius brought the frigate in for the final time, landing it on a nearby plateau. Time for a break.

Having logged out, I stepped away from the computer for a moment to get a drink of water. As I walked through the library, I found two things which surprised me: first, I was high on adrenaline. My heart was beating at overdrive, my hands were shaking, and my breathing was shallow. This wasn't something that had happened to me before, at least not from a video game. Not even *PlanetCrash*. Second, it was dark IRL. This made sense now that I thought about it, since we'd been in that battle for hours. But it hadn't occurred to me until now. I would need a good excuse to feed my parents for why I was out so late...

When I returned to the team, Publius had confirmed from his overhead vantage that we'd cleared the necessary search zone, so we didn't waste time on celebrating. We were all exhausted, anyway, so a few mumbles of "nice work" were all we were up for.

"Since the area is clear of hostiles, we should probably split up," Cubism said, retaking direct command now that the battle was over. "I'll head off in that direction"—he pointed—"Jessica, you're over there; Jeremy, there..." he trailed off as he pointed my direction, obviously as mentally tired as the rest of us. We

56

didn't say anything else, just trudged off in our allotted directions.

The search proved to be slow and boring, a stark contrast to the exhilarating and exhausting battle that had preceded it. Items like the *Armor of Vulnerability* were usually hidden in a small cave or under an overhang, something noticeable enough to check under, but subtle enough that it was unlikely anyone would give them a second thought unless they were looking for them. The challenge was the defenders; the search was busywork to prove you weren't there by accident. My section of the search area held a few candidates which seemed to hold potential as hiding places, but none of them panned out.

When Jeremy finally found the Armor half an hour later, I felt the happiest I'd ever been to *dis*connect from *PlanetCrash*. I needed a nap.

CHAPTER 11

It was past nine o'clock when I finally boarded the monorail back home. I'd always found taking the train after dark to be an almost magical experience. The lights of the city flashed and blurred past the windows, like stars stretched out by faster-than-light travel. Idly, I wondered what that would look like outside of the developer guesswork of *PlanetCrash*, in a real spaceship, with the real laws of physics. In that moment, *PlanetCrash* felt less real, less tangible, less meaningful than it ever had before. In that moment, I dreamed of the real world, and the possibilities that the future could hold.

One of the rare bumps in the ride, where two pieces of track had been imperfectly welded, jolted me out of the moment, and my mind wandered back to *PlanetCrash*. It dawned on me: I'd led a marine drop successfully. I'd *done* it! Was the curse I'd cast on myself back in NA-13 finally lifted? Could I really take command of a squad and not lose a single soldier? It seemed impossible. For so long, I'd simply assumed I wasn't cut out as a leader, but now...

No jumping to conclusions. I'd have to wait and see how the next mission went. If it was the total disaster I was half expecting, I could very well find myself expelled from the project. I prayed that wouldn't happen.

The train glided to a stop at Stony Brook, my home station, and I disembarked. It was only a few blocks from here to...

58

Home. Worry flooded my mind as I realized I'd need an excuse and hadn't come up with one yet. Could I say I'd been on a date? No, they'd never believe that; I needed something at least *a little* plausible. I could hide my wallet outside, say I'd been mugged and, lacking my monorail pass, had to walk home from school? Maybe. It would only take about an hour to walk home though, so I'd need to explain away the others in another way. Besides, my school was in Back Bay, which wasn't exactly in a dangerous area of Boston. Quite the opposite, in fact. Regardless, that excuse wasn't going to work either.

An idea occurred to me: I could tell the truth, but not the whole truth. I'd been at the library. It *sounded* innocent enough. The walk to my house was short and I'd almost arrived. There wouldn't be much time to think of another, unless I wanted to take a lap around the block. I decided against it, choosing instead of walk up to the door and try my luck with my parents.

They were seated silently at the dinner table, heads down, waiting for me as I came inside. My mother was faced away from me, and dad towards. He looked up at me, his eyes red as though he'd been crying. He might well have been; I'd been AWOL for longer than I ever had before. Mom spun around to face me.

"I'm so sorry I'm late, I was…" I didn't make it far into my apology before Dad cut me off.

"The school called," he said, his voice flat, and I broke off halfway through my excuse. *Crap!* That hadn't even occurred to me, even though it was obvious in hindsight. They would have let my parents know as soon as I'd ditched. That had been almost ten hours ago. There would be no getting out of this; I was going to have to face the music.

What followed was their typical lecture, but turned up to eleven. Mom screamed and Dad pretended to try to calm her

59

down in a cheap "good-cop bad-cop" routine from a couple that had watched too many movies.

But their arguments still fell flat, because they were still centered around an axiom that was simply not true: school is more important than *PlanetCrash*. I'd long felt the truth in my heart, but had been unable to justify it in my mind, so I'd gone along with my parents. But Cubism had freed me from that, had shown me that I could build a financially stable life around *PlanetCrash*. The millions I stood to gain in our quest would render meaningless any grades, diplomas, and book learning. My parents would never understand this, though, trapped as they were in the outdated mindset of their youth, that financial success could only be found through education. Maybe they would have a point if we failed our mission. But that hardly seemed likely: no one was trying to stop us, after all.

And while Cubism had freed me from my mental blocks, he had not liberated me from my parents' custody, so when they eventually finished their lecture, they were free to lay down their cold, iron law. My mother informed me that my computer would be removed from my room, that I was grounded, and that I would be banned from *PlanetCrash*. My father, still clinging to his "good cop" role, lightened the punishment, saying that I'd still be allowed to play occasionally, but only under active parental supervision.

This was a threat to the team in *PlanetCrash*, a threat to my ability to contribute to them the level of dedication necessary to remain highly leveled and appropriately available for missions. There was a significant possibility that Cubism would kick me from the team, which represented a hidden threat that my parents did not realize they had given.

My parents were the reason I was in trouble in the first place. With a supportive set of parents, I would be millions of

60

dollars richer in a few months, and would pass it on to them. Even with no parents I'd be better off...

I silently rebuked myself for that stray thought. I knew they meant well, but I wasn't able to take the path they had made for me. Worse, I couldn't even explain why not. They just wouldn't understand, *PlanetCrash* and hacking were way outside their experience.

I silently submitted to their punishments, knowing there was nothing to be gained by standing up for myself. Resistance, no matter how deserved, would only risk alienating Dad from supporting the few rights I was still allowed.

"Is that all?" I asked, eager to be out of there. Dad nodded wearily, and I walked slowly from the room, desperate not to appear as hopeless as I felt. I trudged upstairs and went straight to bed, eager to sleep off the exhaustion both from *PlanetCrash* and my parents.

CHAPTER 12

Twin clouds of gossip and shame hung over me as I came into school the next morning. My departure hadn't exactly been discreet, as I'd essentially sprinted away out the front door. It was an extremely small school as well, so even if no one had seen my flight, my absence would still have been noticed eventually. By now it was common knowledge that I'd fled, but the why of it was utterly mysterious to the rumor mill. And given the way each group would stop talking and stand around awkwardly when I came over to them, it was the hot topic of conversation for the morning.

"Hi, Emily," they'd say as I came over. "How's it going?" This wasn't the harmless question that it usually was, wasn't the conversation starter that we usually used to give each other by way of a generic greeting or leeway to complain about whatever issue bothered us. Today it was different, a pointed inquiry, prying for information that would make anyone who got it popular for the day, the grapevine's toxic reward for feeding it.

I didn't want to play that game. Not today, nor ever. I answered each group in the same way, a terse "fine," that gave no room for follow-up questions. Unfortunately, it had the side effect of killing each conversation, so I was forced to retreat soon after.

For the first time in my high school career, the ring of the first bell came as a relief, a freedom to return to a routine of zoning out.

62

CHAPTER 13

As a result of my punishments for cutting class, I was forced to be offline from *PlanetCrash* until Friday evening. (Note that this did not mean I was getting ahead or even catching up on homework. I just substituted space opera science fiction novels for gaming. From these, I got a crude approximation of the sense of wonder that *PlanetCrash* gave me.)

I'd arranged to do a one-on-one farming session with Val in this time, just as I'd done with Jeremy a few days ago. She hadn't been present for our first mission as a team, so I still knew next to nothing about her playing style.

Val started the private Discord call at the very moment of seven p.m., when we'd arranged to start. It seemed she had been eagerly looking forward to our play session. I connected quickly as well, desperate to get back in-game after my hiatus.

"Hi, Emily!"

That was one thing I already knew about Val before today: her enthusiasm was constant and infectious. Even those two words were said with enough energy that I smiled.

"Heya, Val. How've you been?"

"Oh, I've been good. Busy with school, of course, and it's cut into my time in *PlanetCrash*, which sucks, and I missed the mission for it—how'd that go?—but I'm excited to be back and with you!" Val spoke quickly, her voice tinged with the accent of a North American whose native language was Spanish.

63

"The mission went well…" I began, but she cut me off almost immediately.

"Oh, I know, Cubism told me, you got the item! I don't know why I asked, I wasn't thinking I guess, but good work! I'm glad we're off to a good start!"

"So…" I began, "should we get started on playing?"

"Oh, yeah, yes! I just unlocked my first DMR last night; I haven't gotten a chance to use it yet and I'm dying to try it out." She paused for the first time. "What level are you? I'm only at six right now, I hope we aren't too different?"

"Eight," I replied. "Should be workable."

"I'll make it happen! I'll bring the Val A-game, I'll hit every shot, I'll be a force of nature! You don't have to worry about me, Emily, I won't slow you down!"

"I'm sure of it," I said, not wanting to upset her. "But we should start out with an easier mission, as a warm-up. It's what I did with Jeremy, too."

A faint sigh of relief, barely audible, floated through the the call. Unless I'd imagined it?

"That works too, I guess, I mean, of course I could keep up and don't need to but if you want to warm up we can warm up!"

I'd had far more than my fill of Almanac while levelling alone and with Jeremy, so I was in no hurry to go back. "Do you want to head out to Orisa-B?" I suggested. "There's lower level opportunities there and we cleared most of the high-level stuff during the last mission anyway. Should be relatively safe now, for a few days at least."

Val gave her assent, and we departed for the Orisa system. Lacking Publius' piloting skills and spaceship, we were relegated to having to fly on a commercial spaceflight between systems.

64

Our personal craft could manage short-range, interplanetary travel, but not a cross-galaxy jump like this.

Commercial travel was designed to feel uncomfortable. No matter how few players bought tickets for a given cross-galactic spaceflight, the game would always insert enough NPCs to make the flight crowded, claustrophobic. So Val and I ended up squeezed together on a starship that had maybe one other real person on it. We weren't interacting with anyone, though, so it was impossible to say for sure.

Val's avatar was a tall, strong woman with long and flowing auburn hair. Was that what Val herself looked like? I assumed not based on her voice: I'd imagined her as small. But I didn't really know for sure.

During the flight, we talked about ourselves.

Val had just begun high school recently, last month, in fact, but she was already incredibly stressed about it. Her parents, it seemed, wouldn't accept anything less than perfection from her. A ninety-eight out of one hundred was failure to them.

I could only partially relate. We both were buckling under the expectations placed upon us by our parents, but her bar was much higher. My parents just wanted me to graduate and go to college, not ace every test. Fortunately for Val, it seemed her capacities were more suited to her parents' expectations than mine and she largely kept them happy. It simply came with a high mental cost to Val. I wondered if her parents knew what they were doing to her.

With the hope that it might allay some of her stress, I shared my academic failure with her. I was, of course, barely passing in school. Any interest I might've had in learning any of the subjects was killed by the structure of it. Sure, there were cool parts of History, but my teachers seemed desperate to overshadow it with forcing the memorization of dates and timelines.

65

And my lack of interest had compounded upon my first road-block, leading to the pathetic failure I was today.

We really didn't have much in common, it turned out, besides *PlanetCrash*. There was an incredibly visceral sense of satisfaction we shared, the dopamine release of a headshot, the adrenaline rush of combat, and the mental satisfaction of knowing that you'd beaten your opponent. Those were possible in most video games, though. What elevated *PlanetCrash* was the immersion, the feeling that you were really there, the strategic and tactical layer formed beyond simply getting headshots, and the beauty of a world that was not confined to a single planet.

About halfway through the flight, the NPC pilot announced that we'd be decelerating soon. It was an inevitability on transgalactic flights. Most craft simply didn't have the fuel capacity to make it in a single jump and those that did were quite expensive. So the majority of flights would stop once or twice to refuel. The fact that we'd made it this far already suggested that we'd only need one stop.

We dropped down into sublight speeds, but shuddered with an impact just as we did. Instantly alert, I peeked out the window for any clue as to what was going on. It wasn't much of a mystery: I could clearly see through the window that we'd been trapped in a space net. These were the tools of both player characters and NPC pirates, designed to catch ships just like ours unawares as they dropped from lightspeed near fueling stations. The route from Almanac to this fuel depot must have been a common route, because the sheer vastness of space meant that outside of the most heavily trafficked areas, it would be nigh impossible to catch anything.

I snapped into focus, readying the autoshotgun I'd acquired on my mission with Jeremy. It would be perfect for fighting in the confines of a spaceship.

66

"We're caught in a net," I told Val. "Get ready to get boarded."

Briefly, I worried about how she'd fare. Close quarters was not the fight you brought a sharpshooter to. But I had to dismiss the thought. I'd have enough to worry about when the boarding began.

The entry and escape hatches burst open on all sides of the passenger compartment. "Everyone on the ground, now!" one of the pirates shouted. The NPCs began to comply, the obedient sheep that they were. Val and I, on the other hand, opened fire.

Val's first shot was on the money, right between the eyes of the pirate who'd ordered us to bite the dirt. I didn't have time to watch her after that, though: more pirates were swarming aboard.

My auto-shotgun blasts ripped through the NPCs, seats, and pirates, thickening the spaceship's air with blood and dusty upholstery. As that fallout began to settle, and my weapon to overheat, I bolted towards the bathroom at the back and took cover within. While I ran, the pirates unloaded their pulse rifles, flatlining the remaining NPCs that had survived my initial burst of fire. The entire interior of the spaceship glowed green with the light of a thousand laser blasts. A few stray shots pierced the bathroom walls, but not enough to deplete my shields. I leaned out for a moment to return fire, adding the purple of my plasma shotgun to the light show. It was impossible to see anything through the mess of the firefight, so I aimed more or less randomly. As my gun began to overheat again, I returned to my hiding place in the bathroom.

In that moment, though, I knew that I was screwed. I'd given away my position, hit them for everything I'd had, but the fire was still relentless. I couldn't even tell the difference

67

from before I'd fired, so large was their pirate gang. I couldn't die here, though, I *wouldn't!*

A thought struck me. The plasma autoshotgun wasn't the only loot I'd picked up with Jeremy. I still had grenades. They were expensive, but if I died here I'd never get a chance to use them anyway. In such a confined space, I figured one fragmentation grenade would be enough. After a moment's hesitation, though, I equipped two. If one wasn't enough, they'd charge me down before I had a chance to get the second one off.

I pulled the pins and tossed the frags out of the bathroom and into the cabin. And it was then, just a second too late, that I remembered about Val. She was still out there!

"Cover!" I shouted to her, hoping she still had enough time to react.

The two explosions were so close together that they melded into one, flinging everything in the cabin into the outer walls. The bathroom stall door wasn't steel, just thin aluminum, so it only protected me from some of the shrapnel. My shields broke from the damage, but I didn't take enough loss in HP to actually die. I knew I'd be better off than anyone else in there, though, due having at least some protection, so I raised my shotgun and stepped out, ready to finish off any survivors. I saw none.

The 'disconnect' sound played in Discord: Val had hung up on me. My heartrate shot far above where it had been even in the height of the firefight. I pulled up my killfeed, my hand shaking, to confirm what I'd already realized: I'd killed Val with my grenades.

My heart sank faster than my character's level rose. The exp from the dozens of kills I'd just racked up poured in, levelling me up from 8 to 10, but it was negligible next to the amount by which I'd set us back. Val had been lagging behind us before because of school and her absence on our first mission, but I'd just reset her entirely. It would take ages for her to recover.

Guilt began to settle on my shoulders. If I'd held back on the grenades, used only one, she might have survived. Hell, the only reason we'd travelled at all was because I was *bored* of Almanac. If I'd been more patient, kept us in safer territory, she would have survived. *If she'd found good cover, she would have survived!* a voice in my head shouted back. I blocked it out. It was a voice that continually refused to take responsibility for my actions, for the people that fell under my command.

Cubism was online on Discord, so I called him up.

He responded after a few seconds. "What's up, Emily?"

"Val's dead," I said bluntly, not wanting to beat around the bush. "I blew her up by accident in a firefight with pirates."

Cubism cursed. "You're still alive, though, right?"

"Yeah, and the area seems clear. I should be able to make it out."

"Okay. Loot her body and anything else in the area. I'll put the word out to find a replacement."

"A what…a *replacement*?" I was incredulous. "You're dropping her?"

"We can't afford to carry deadweight," he replied. "We'll get someone who's at level with the rest of us, don't worry."

He paused for a moment. "Don't make a habit of teamkilling, by the way, or you won't be worth your weight on this team either."

"I don't…" I began, but Cubism had already disconnected from the call.

I looted the spacecraft and disembarked before quitting out of *PlanetCrash* to think.

My emotions were jumbled. Cubism's firing of Val only compounded the guilt I felt at killing her, but all the same I was perversely relieved that he'd taken out his anger on her and not me. I'd have to make sure to stay on his good side in the future, or I could end up kicked to the curb as easily as Val.

CHAPTER 14

I'd stayed closely in touch with Jeremy after our one-on-one farm session and we'd been chatting every evening in the past week. I knew he'd find out about Val soon enough, through Jessica if not Cubism, so I decided to let him know first. It wasn't the most fun way to start our chat that evening, but was necessary.

```
I killed Val.
```

He took only a few minutes to respond.

```
like irl or what? cuz if its irl im gonna have
to call the fuzz on ya
```

I couldn't help but laugh despite my guilt.

```
This isn't funny. I teamkilled her while we
were trying to farm together and now Cubism is
kicking her from the team.
```

```
he's kicking her? jesus.
```

```
Yeah apparently she's too far behind.
"Deadweight" was the term he used.
```

```
:/
```

```
Told me to watch my back too
```

```
whatcha mean?
```

71

```
He said if I teamkill again he'll drop me. I
know that's not unreasonable, it's just scary
to be one mistake away from being dropped.
```

```
yea. im gonna start treading carefully myself.
doesnt seem theres a lot of job security here.
```

The subject shifted from there. Jeremy's job interview had gone well, he felt, and he'd find out next week whether he'd gotten the position. That said, he didn't think he would take it: with Cubism's willingness to cut people from the project, Jeremy felt a day job would only serve as a distraction from the multi-million dollar payout we expected from the project. I wondered if he would have taken the job and dropped from our crazy project if it hadn't been for his father's death. It didn't seem like it'd help to ask, though.

He turned the conversation to my life.

```
so, you haven't dropped school yet?
```

```
What do you mean "yet"? I'm not going to...
```

```
im just saying, im worried a job will
interfere, and jobs dont even have homework.
```

```
Not like I do my homework anyway, lol
```

```
then why are you even in school? youre halfway
dropped out already, just gotta finalize it.
```

```
It's just not gonna work for me.
```

I was a little annoyed the Jeremy kept pushing this topic on me. If I dropped, my parents would never let me play *Planet-Crash* again.

```
I gotta find the balance that actually
maximizes my playtime, ya know?
```

```
i guess.
```

He seemed unconvinced, but let the issue go.

72

We talked a while longer before he left to get dinner.

CHAPTER 15

My phone woke me early Sunday morning, at nine a.m. It was a message from Cubism: our next mission! I bolted upright and out of bed. My parents would just be starting church, so I had at least an hour or two before they'd be home. Hopefully, this mission wouldn't go on as long as the last.

I sprinted to the computer, not bothering to get dressed. Cubism and Jessica were already online: it seemed she'd located another of the items we needed. I connected to our voice chat.

"What's the situation?" I asked.

"I'll explain once everyone's here," Jessica replied sharply, her usual cold self. "For now, just meet us at these coordinates."

"On my way." I launched *PlanetCrash* and jumped into my ship. Fortunately, I was close to the coordinates. I wouldn't be the one we waited on.

Jeremy connected a few minutes later, just as I was arriving at the rendezvous point. As with me, his welcome from Jessica was cool and business-like. Jeremy's arrival was closely followed by a new name, one I hadn't seen before. I tensed up, suspecting who this was.

Before long, a new figure was standing before me, a short but intimidating woman who'd spent EC to customize her character into a colorful theme for her armor that contrasted dramatically with Jeremy's all-black look. I'd always thought of that sort of customization as wasteful pageantry, but I did have

74

to admit her character looked amazing. The deep brown of her skin provided a beautiful base for the bright greens and oranges of her armor, the same colors as the *PlanetCrash* logo.

"Oh, good, you're here," Cubism greeted the newcomer. "Everyone, this is Marissa Washington. She's Val's replacement."

"Hey, everyone." Marissa's voice was strong, radiating power from even such a simple greeting. She turned her avatar towards mine. "I hear you're the reason I'm here. I owe you one." Her tone indicated light mockery, not truly thankful nor accusatory: just friendly banter.

I chuckled sheepishly, not wanting to discuss the incident. "I guess so."

Pulling up Marissa's profile and equipment gave me more information about her. As she was Val's replacement, I'd anticipated that she would be a sharpshooter, and her items confirmed this. She had a diverse collection of high-level sniper rifles and DMRs and a single pulse rifle for close quarters combat. Her character was level 12, higher even than Jeremy, who was the next highest in the team at 11. I was glad I'd reached 10. Being back at 8 still would have just been embarrassing. Marissa's good equipment didn't necessarily mean high-skill though, and I'd take Val's deadeye accuracy over high-level weapons any day. It is a far easier task to level up your character and equipment than your real-life abilities.

Jessica's briefing began shortly after Publius' arrival and our introduction to Marissa.

"We've located the next item necessary for our project. It was listed as part of the bounty stolen from the Legion of Honor, one of the larger kingdoms on the server. Pirates hit their transport fleet last week and a few days ago the LoH posted an open letter in which they noted everything that had been stolen, demanded its return, and swore revenge. The item we're

75

after is the Burning Rifle. As the name suggests, it has an in-game effect that it sets the target on fire. Fifty extra damage per second. The rifle is small potatoes compared to most of the other stuff on the list, but it's the only thing we care about. Everything else we'll return to the Legion."

"We're giving it back?" Publius asked. "Wouldn't it be beneficial to keep everything?"

"In the short term, yes, it would be," Cubism replied. "But there's a diplomatic angle to this as well. If we keep the loot, the LoH might not care, or they might put their sights on us. We don't know. However, if we return it, we could have a powerful friend in the future for assistance in securing some of the rarer items. I've already been in contact with one of their lieutenants, who said we're free to keep the Burning Rifle if we track down and return the other stuff, plus he'll keep an eye out for our other items."

"You gave him the list?" I was incredulous. "What if he figures out what we're doing? A kingdom as powerful as the Legion could easily beat us to these items!"

"Not the full thing. Just the items with Legendary rarity."

"Gotcha." On reflection, it was a smart move. Common and rare items we'd be able to get pretty easily on our own: in fact, Publius and Jessica had added a few to our collection since the last mission. We only went out in force for items with high enough rarity that we couldn't just count on running into them randomly. A list of legendary items would be less suspicious to Cubism's contact and they were the ones where the resources of a group like the Legion of Honor would really pay dividends. Plus a vastly incomplete list would prevent anyone, no matter what they knew about computer security, from determining the true purpose of our hunt.

Jessica resumed her control of the meeting, eager to retake the reins of power. "I've been working to track down the pirates ever since I picked this up. Now I know where they are."

She paused. A map of the galaxy appeared in-game in the center of the room in which we were meeting. Jessica gestured with her avatar. "They're lying in wait along this hyperlane here, just outside of fueling station Alpha-469, which is here. They'll wait for a sufficiently good catch, then ambush and board. Pretty standard pirate tactics."

"Won't we be sitting ducks? If they're prepared to ambush someone coming out of a hyperlane, how do we get the jump on them? I get that we have an advantage by knowing they're there, but..." Marissa trailed off, her point made.

"We don't have to come from the hyperlane," Publius responded. "If we come from the neighboring system here"—he gestured to a nearby star—"we can come at them from the side. They won't be expecting to be flanked. We need to check if we'll have enough fuel though. What's the distance between these?"

Jessica played with the map for a moment. "Five light-years."

"I don't want to rely on the fueling station there, though," Marissa interjected. "In case we need to bug out in a hurry."

There was a moment of silence while Publius calculated. "Yeah, we should be good to go on that."

"Boarding is the next issue," I said. This was my domain, my area of expertise. "We can't just blow up their ship and risk destroying the item. Publius, can you get us close enough to board safely?"

"Yeah," he replied. "I'll have to stay with the ship though. Is everyone else going on the boarding party?"

"We stand a better chance with more people," I said. "I think Jeremy should take point, if everyone's *on board* for that?"

Groans at my pun were followed by murmurs of assent, so I continued. "Once we have a visual on the enemy ship, we'll see if we have time to identify it while we close in. Most pirates use prebuilt rather than custom ships, so we might be able to pull blueprints for the interior if we're quick enough. That'll be invaluable. Unless you've got that info already?" I directed the question to Jessica, who shook her head.

"Time to get into the cockpit," Cubism instructed Publius. "We'll discuss the rest of the finer details of the boarding during the flight."

With that the flight and the mission began. We went over specific tactics en route: I would use my automatic shotgun again (the massive spread of which meant I needed to be directly behind Jeremy, to minimize risks of friendly fire). Jessica had a shotgun of her own, equipped with a comically large suppressor. It was more easily controlled than my automatic, but had a lower fire rate, so she would be third in our line of battle, directly behind me. Marissa would follow her, equipping her one of her faster-firing DMRs. Conventional wisdom would have preferred her pulse rifle for its even higher fire rate, but being so far back in the group meant she would have to take careful aim to avoid hitting us anyway, so the increased per-shot damage of the DMR would pay off. Cubism took up the rear, the standard for any commanding officer in *PlanetCrash* joining his troops on a mission.

Our debates over order and gear lasted most of the flight. It wasn't long after we'd settled matters that Publius gave his call out: "We're sixty seconds out from the drop to sublight speeds."

I could feel every vibration of the ship in those moments, despite sitting in a chair on earth. My brain didn't recognize

78

that. It clung firmly to the belief that I stood in a spaceship, headed into battle.

The motion and associated rattling noises ceased as we dropped from lightspeed. I became acutely aware of my own heavy breath, pressured by the typical pre-mission nerves.

"Uhh, Cubism? We've got a problem here," Publius said, breaking the silence.

"Say again?" Cubism replied. "Bit of static on my end of the channel, sorry."

"We have a problem. There's two hostile vessels, not just one."

"Publius, can you take one out in a dogfight after the rest of us board the other?" Marissa asked.

"Negative." Jessica didn't give Publius a chance to respond. "We don't have intel on which ship has the asset. We can't risk destroying it. If we're going to do that, we might as well just go home now, save ourselves the risk."

"We don't have time to argue about this," Publius said. "We either need to go in or get out before they notice us. We're on a clock here."

"There's only two options," I spoke up. "Either we give up and go home, or we split into two boarding parties. I can lead one, of course, and Jeremy can get the other. One with me, I think Marissa, and then Jessica and Cubism go with Jeremy. The call's up to Cube, though, if we're going to abort."

"Let's do it," Cubism said. "Publius, take us in."

"Aye aye. I can't stay with the first boarding party, though, so you'll have nowhere to retreat to if things go south."

"No problem," I replied with far more confidence than I felt. "Marissa and I will take that one."

"You really are trying to get me killed, aren't you?" Marissa laughed.

79

I didn't acknowledge it. I still wasn't ready to joke about that. "Let's get into position at the airlock."

"I'll give you a shout when we're about to attach to the target," Publius said. "You'll only have a couple seconds to get on board. I'll need to head straight over to the other ship, we won't have time to dawdle."

We donned combat space suits in the airlock. There was a significant chance when trying to latch onto a hostile craft that you'd get spaced and you needed to be prepared for that. At the same time, a full Apollo Mission-style spacesuit was impossible to fight in. The combat suits were a poor imitation of both traditional space suits and body armor. They weren't great protection from bullets *or* from the vacuum, but they were the only thing that could even try to save you from both at once.

"Thirty seconds to drop off." The callout from Publius came just as Marissa and I finished getting our suits on.

I hit the switch to depressurize the airlock. It would be one less step to implement when docking began.

The ship shuddered as Publius rammed into the pirates. It was impossible to get a soft docking with hostile spacecraft, so you just went in hard and hoped for the best.

"Go, go, go!" Cubism shouted.

I threw open the outer door of the airlock, then hopped across onto the pirates' ship. Marissa followed just a step behind. Publius hadn't been able to perfectly align us with the pirates' airlock, so we clung to its ridge. We'd be able to pull ourselves in once Publius drew away and our own airlock was no longer blocking our entry.

The pirates had noticed the collision, though, of course, and fired their thrusters before Publius had a chance to undock. The two spaceships scraped against each other before coming free, and Publius reacted, punching the prograde boosters up to full power, knowing he only had a few moments to catch the other hostile. As our airlock flew by, though, it clipped my head, and I lost my grip on the pirates' ship. My heart accelerated and breath went short as I was knocked free from both ships, spaced between them.

Marissa noticed almost immediately and reached out her avatar's arm to me. It was already too late though and I was out of reach. A death sentence for me. Publius might try get the ship back before my oxygen ran out, but that would jeaopardize the mission.

"Don't worry about me, get on board!" I called out.

"What's going on?" Cubism asked.

"I'm spaced. Don't come back for me, though, get to the other ship! I'll deal with this."

Both Publius and Marissa obeyed, keeping the mission in the forefront of their priorities. Publius kept his thrusters on max and Marissa equipped her breaching charge, sticking it to the outer door of the airlock. A soundless ball of flame emanated from the breach charge as Marissa detonated it and she dove into the airlock just as much of the air from inside the ship flew out with its depressurization. One of the crew flew out with it, due to the pressure change, leaving him spaced like I was. I equipped my rifle and shot him twice, just to make sure he didn't have a lifeline that I hadn't seen.

The team's radio chatter echoed emptily in my ears as they boarded the second ship.

With no air, gravity, or friction to resist, the force my gunshots had propelled me backwards, and I floated further away from any of the ships. An idea struck me. Could I use my rifle to propel myself back to the airlock? I peered towards it, trying to picture the angles in my head. It'd take at least two shots: I didn't have a clear path to the airlock at the moment. I angled my rifle and fired the first shot, which sent me floating in the right direction to give me a direct path to the airlock. I spun a

81

hundred-and-eighty degrees and fired a second shot once I was correctly aligned: this canceled out the momentum of the first, leaving me perfectly positioned. I aimed my rifle directly away from the airlock and fired, over and over to close the gap more quickly. I wanted to be able to support Marissa as soon as possible.

I flew through the open airlock and smacked directly into a pirate who'd been trying to flank Marissa from the stern of the ship. He was, of course, far more surprised than I, and I took his few moments of hesitation to spray my rifle directly into his head.

Now that I was on board, I took a moment to get my footing and re-equip my automatic shotgun. Then I charged towards the bow to support Marissa. The ship wasn't large, and I arrived at the helm in just a few seconds. Marissa was covered behind an instrumentation panel, pinned down by fire from three pirates. Three pirates who, it seemed, were focused entirely on her, and failed to notice the backup charging down the corridor. I opened fire with my automatic shotgun just before entering the helm, blasting all three of the pirates down before they had a chance to react.

"Helm is clear," I reported, in the most calm and professional voice I could muster, trying to hide the exhilaration I was feeling.

"That's all hostiles down over here," Marissa replied. "Target one is secure, we're going to start searching for the asset."

There were grunts of confirmation from the other boarding team, who, it seemed, were still embroiled in their own firefight.

Our search was both uneventful and unsuccessful. We were unable to find the Burning Rifle, but we collected the remaining loot for delivery back to the Legion of Honor.

A few minutes later, after Jeremy and his team secured and searched their ship, they reported the same. The Burning Rifle was nowhere to be found. Publius picked us up, and we all met aboard our own ship to discuss.

"Can you show me a list of what you found?" Jessica asked. She seemed tense, perhaps worried that the Burning Rifle's failure to appear where she'd predicted it would reflect poorly on her.

"Sure."

Moments ticked by while Jessica examined the lists we provided for her.

"It's pretty clear cut, I guess," she said eventually. "I cross-referenced what we found on both ships with what the LoH reported as missing. We've only got about two-thirds of the items. There must be a third ship that wasn't with the first two."

There were no objections: none of us had a better theory.

Jessica sighed. "I'll get to work on this. You'll hear from me once I find the third ship. In the meantime, Cubism, you'll probably want to turn over the items we have found to the LoH."

"I don't think I should, actually," he responded. "They might think we're withholding things from them if we show up with only two-thirds of their loot. Let's wait to contact them until we've found the whole set."

He paused before addressing the rest of us. "You guys did good work. I know that this ended up being a wild-goose chase, but we didn't take any casualties, plus we all got some exp and EC. I'll call it a win." A hard tone crept into his voice. "Assuming Jessica can find us the last ship."

"I will," she said earnestly. "I promise."

Cubism disconnected from the server without another word. I took that as a dismissal and followed him out, worried that my parents would be home any second.

CHAPTER 16

I returned to school on Monday fairly satisfied that my life had stabilized. I'd put enough time into *PlanetCrash* Sunday morning that I felt able to take the rest of the day off, which pleased my parents to no end. Playing *less* than the amount they'd allowed? Clearly their discipline had paid off!

My parent's strategy hadn't, of course, had anything to do with my use of my time, but I'd encouraged that thinking, and even had done all of my homework for the weekend. Not well, of course, but at least I had *something* that I could turn in. It wasn't going to fix my GPA, but it wasn't going to get me called out in front of the class again.

Inevitably, it was just at this peak when everything began to well and truly crash down.

The chaos began with a simple buzz of my phone during Latin class. It was, of course, banned to check your phone during class, but that never stopped anyone except for the absolute teachers' pets.

My heart sank when I saw the sender: Cubism.

```
Jessica found target #3. We need to move
immediately. Get in here ASAP.
```

I couldn't go, I knew that. Skipping out of school again would undo everything I'd accomplished this weekend, would almost certainly get me banned from *PlanetCrash* entirely and indefinitely. To go in now would hold back the bigger project

85

far more than my missing this one event. Cubism would understand, though. I hoped.

My phone buzzed again a few minutes later. Another message from Cubism.

```
Where are you?
```

Again, I ignored it, but my level of stress rose even higher.

A third message followed later. I didn't even read it.

Cubism didn't reach out to me again, but I didn't calm down. The rest of the day I spent on edge, my heart racing and breath short. I didn't usually absorb much at school, but this day was worse than usual. I couldn't recall a single word from that day, not even a minute after they were spoken.

I called Cubism, breathless, as soon as I got out of my last class for the day.

"Hi, Emily." As usual, his voice betrayed nothing of his feelings. It wasn't comforting.

"I'm sorry about today," I said quickly. "I was in school; I can't skip out again or my parents will kill me, they'll ban me from playing *PlanetCrash*, I won't be able to contribute at all. It's better this way, for the group..."

"Emily," he began as I trailed off. "I honestly don't give a damn about your personal problems. I took you on to do a job and if you won't do the job, I'll have to find someone else. Maybe if you were exceptionally good at your job, I'd consider keeping you on 'part-time.' But you're not. You killed Val. You abandoned Marissa for most of the mission yesterday. You didn't come today; you're not dedicated. You're becoming more of a liability than an asset and I can't afford to drag deadweight and then pay you millions for holding us back. You either need to find a way to meet expectations, or get out of my way."

"I'll...I'll find a way."

86

"Find it quickly." He hung up on me, leaving me shocked. I didn't know what I was going to do. My only options seemed to be either continuing as I was until Cubism kicked me, or giving up now and resigning, leaving with my head held high.

I walked to the Public Garden while considering the possibilities. Neither was appealing, so I called Jeremy for advice.

After recapping my conversation with Cubism to him, he explained that the answer was obvious. "It's like I told you before: you gotta drop out of school."

"It's like *I* told *you* before! My parents are not going to accept that!" I was nearly shouting, drawing a few glances from passers-by. The Public Garden wasn't where people usually had their angry phone calls.

"Well, there's a solution for that too," he replied calmly.

"What do you mean?"

"Don't you see? Your parents are just holding you back. They want you to grow up, go to college, get a job in the system, and never accomplish anything *real*. You can't let them stop you."

"What do you mean? I live with them, there's no way around that…"

He laughed quietly, a humorless, sympathetic sound. "I'm pretty sure you'll know when you're ready."

"The hell do you mean by that, Jeremy?"

"Exactly what I said," he responded. "Think on it for a while. I have faith the solution will come to you. Feel free to call me again when it does, we can discuss it. Talk to you later?"

I sighed, more confused than I had been when we'd started talking. "Yeah, I guess so."

He hung up, leaving me to wander the Public Garden with my thoughts.

It was a good place to think, at least. I idled over to the bridge which spanned the lagoon at the center of the Garden, resting up against the guardrails to reflect on what Jeremy had said.

He'd seemed to think there was an obvious way out of this, something staring me in the face that I was simply unable to see. I ran through the situation again in my head. If I stayed in school, Cubism would kick me off the team. If I dropped out like Jeremy had, my parents would kill me and then Cubism would kick me off the team anyway. There was no room for a third option here, no way to both stay in and drop out, and no way to do neither.

Perhaps there *was* a third option, though. There was a way to leave school without dropping out: graduating. Of course, I couldn't meet my school's requirements soon enough, as they were listed in terms of "years of study." "Four years of English," for example, was not a requirement I could fulfill in two years. So I'd have to work outside the system. A GED? It was a possibility. I'd still have to wait for a test date, though, and somehow get the hundreds of dollars necessary to pay for it. My parents wouldn't go along with this if I proposed it to them, but they might if I asked forgiveness instead of permission...

I'd still need to leave school right away to stay in *Planet-Crash*. It also seemed unlikely that I'd be able to afford the test until after receiving the payout from our heist.

So I'd need to not only stay out of school until the end of our mission, but also stay away from my parents. I mentally froze for a moment as the idea sunk in, my heartrate accelerating past the speed of sound. This must have been the solution that Jeremy had referenced: leaving both school *and* home, so that neither of them could enforce their rules upon me. I could play *PlanetCrash* at the library: I'd done it before and while it

88

wasn't ideal, I could still perform at a high level without the comfort of my home PC.

Finding a place to live would be a hassle. The city provided "subsidized housing units," where anyone who was down on their luck could move into a room to stay in, no questions asked. It was part of a "housing first" policy initiative from a few years back. The subsidized housing units were super crappy, I'd heard, but they were safe, warm and free, which was all I really needed. I'd worry about comfort once I was rolling in the millions from Cubism's payout. I couldn't go to one too close to home, though, as my parents might check it...

With that thought, the insanity of what I was actually *considering* began to hit me. Running away from home? Was I crazy?

What was the alternative, though? Cubism had offered me something incredible. A chance I'd never had before: to pursue what I loved instead of suffering through what I hated. I'd always believed my parents before, when they'd said that I'd need to do well in school to do well in life, and it had filled me with dread. Now I had a chance to be free: to follow my passion.

The decision crystalized in my mind. I'd do it. I'd leave tonight. I'd fully commit to Cubism. It was time.

CHAPTER 17

Hiding my plans from my parents that evening was an issue I hadn't anticipated. I was nervous and jittery throughout dinner and afterward, which raised their suspicions that *something* was afoot. Fortunately, they couldn't tell what, and didn't press me on it. So they went to sleep mildly worried instead of going totally ballistic, as they would have been if I'd spilled. Which I might have. Confrontation is hard.

I usually stayed up later than my parents, well past midnight, so the fact that I was still awake when they went to bed didn't further their concerns. After waiting another hour to be sure they were deep asleep, though, I began to pack.

Traveling light was a necessity. I'd have to personally carry everything and could only walk with so much. Basic necessities, like food, were provided at the housing units, so I wouldn't need to take those into account. I threw what I needed into my backpack and snuck downstairs. I knew that the fourth stair from the bottom squeaked and while it was almost certainly not going to be loud enough to wake my parents, I didn't want to risk it. I stepped directly over it instead. I dropped a note on the table, explaining that I was okay without giving away where I was going. With that done, I opened a window and hopped out into the night, avoiding the ungreased hinges on all the doors outside.

It was a little past one a.m., not so late that the monorails had stopped running yet, so I headed to the nearest Orange Line station. My destination was the housing unit in Andrew Square, part of South Boston. I'd chosen it for a few reasons: first, it was fairly far away from home. My parents might check the local ones, but they couldn't search every housing unit in Boston hoping to run into me. Second, it was easily accessible to the rapid transit system. The Red Line, which had a stop in Andrew Square, hadn't been upgraded from subway to monorail yet, but it was still a great way to get around the city: only less comfortable. Finally, Jeremy lived in Southie. I didn't know exactly where, but even being in the area gave me some comfort.

A pang of guilt hit as I sat on the train. My parents wouldn't know what had happened to me: I'd simply have disappeared when they woke up in the morning. Should I have left a longer explanation? It didn't matter: it was too late now anyway. There was no going back there, not until our heist was completed and I was a millionaire.

I gazed out the window. There wasn't much that I could see at this time of night, when it was dark outside and bright on the train, but the occasional lit building shone through the blackness. I idly wondered what the people in those buildings were doing at this hour. Working late? Having an affair? Playing *PlanetCrash*?

The train drifted into Downtown Crossing, which was the connection between the Orange and Red lines. The transition from monorail to subway wasn't one I'd done much, as I didn't usually have cause to take the Red line anywhere. Two flights of stairs took me down to the Red, first from the elevated monorail to the street level, then the second into the subway tunnels.

Riding the Red Line was far less pleasant than the Orange. The train was louder, rougher, and the enclosed subway tunnels were tight and claustrophobic. Andrew wasn't far down the line, though, with only two intervening stops. I disembarked the train and headed back up the stairs to see my new neighborhood.

This was a fairly run-down area, a far cry from the glistening glass skyscrapers of the Back Bay or even the rows of well-maintained middle-class homes that I was used to in Jamaica Plain. Southie was one of the few parts of the city that hadn't modernized to the twenty-first century yet. Still, the streets near Andrew Square were well lit even at night and I made it to the Subsidized Housing Unit without any trouble. It was a tall brick building, wide enough that it covered about half of its block. A single lightbulb burned in the entrance, illuminating a desk where a doorman sat.

I entered the building and the man looked up at me vaguely. "You need a room?" he asked.

"I guess so, yeah."

"Name?" he asked. I hesitated. "You can make one up if you want. I just need to log that the room is taken."

"Gart Gasper," I said, borrowing the name of my NA-21 *PlanetCrash* character.

"That's a stupid name. Third floor," he said bluntly, throwing a key at me. I dropped it, too surprised to react in time. He snorted with laughter. I scooped the key off the ground, placing it in my pocket, then mumbled a thanks and fled to the stairs to head up to my new housing.

Reaching the third floor, I realized that I didn't know which room was mine. I thought about returning downstairs to ask the doorman, but decided I'd save that as a last resort. I didn't want to talk to him again if avoidable. I pulled the key from my pocket to see if there'd be any hint. Indeed there was: the number '327' was engraved on the side. A feeling of stupidity washed over me, but it was quickly drowned out by the relief that I wouldn't need to interact with the guy downstairs again. I started down the hall, checking the numbers on each door I passed. Quite a ways down, almost at the end of the hallway, was 327. I unlocked the door and pushed it open. My new home was a small, single room, furnished only with an old mattress on the floor. I'd passed both bathroom and a kitchen area in the hallways, so it was clear that those were shared facilities. The kitchen had seemed a little small, but I didn't know how many of the rooms on this floor were even occupied. Hopefully, they weren't filled to capacity.

I dropped my backpack to the ground and let myself fall onto the mattress, the physical and emotional exhaustion of the day catching up to me.

Before I could go to sleep, though, there were two messages I had to send.

First to Cubism:

```
I found a way. You'll have no more problems
with me.
```

Second, to Jeremy:

```
The solution came to me, like you said. I'll
call you in the morning if you want.
```

Then I turned off my phone and sank into the mattress to sleep.

CHAPTER 18

The next morning I woke up early, my brain still so hard-wired for high school that I didn't even need an alarm. A confusing mix of emotions washed over me: doubt about whether I'd made the right decision; anxiety about the stress I must have caused my parents; excitement at taking control of my own life for the first time; and relief that despite being up so early, I wouldn't need to go to school. In fact, I'd never need to do that again. I groped around for my phone and checked the time and my notifications. It was 6:30 a.m., my usual wake-up time for school. That was a habit I was ready to break.

Cubism hadn't responded to my message yet, so I guessed he kept a better sleep schedule than I did. Jeremy, on the other hand, had: timestamped at just a half-hour after my original message. I'd been dead asleep by then, though.

```
i knew youd work it out. youre a smart cookie.
call me whenever.
```

There was a follow-up message about forty-five minutes after:

```
im gonna hit the hay actually, i guess you
already did as well. dont call before 10, ill
be asleep.
```

That gave me three and a half hours to kill before he'd be awake.

I noticed a card taped to the back of my door. It had probably been there since I'd arrived and I just hadn't realised. It detailed the basic information about living here: where to get necessities like soap and clothing; when they'd provide hot meals; and some resources for finding jobs in the area. The latter, I wouldn't need, of course, as *PlanetCrash* would be my full-time job until Cubism's payout allowed me to retire. But the others would still be useful. Breakfast apparently ran from six through nine, so I headed downstairs to eat.

There were maybe twenty people in the soup kitchen, which took up most of the first floor of the building. Two choices as to where to sit faced me. Taking up most of the room were a couple of long tables linked with backless benches. That was one option. The other was to sit at one of a few smaller tables, that could seat maybe six, were off to the sides. Their purpose was apparent from the woman who was sitting at one trying to wrangle with her three children: a space for families. Most everyone else was sat at the middle tables.

The majority of people there were in groups and seemed to know each other already. It was a diverse crowd and ages seemed to range from a boy who couldn't be much older than I was to a woman who seemed to be pushing a hundred.

I wasn't sure which of the groups I'd fit in to. Probably none. I grabbed food and sat alone. There was no rush to eat, as the library wouldn't open until 9 a.m. anyway. It'd take about half an hour to get there on the train, so I wouldn't have to leave until 8:30. That gave me two more hours before I could start my day in *PlanetCrash*. I was eager to, though, as the others had undoubtedly been levelling like crazy in my absence.

A few minutes into my meal, Cubism responded to my text from the previous night..

```
Glad to hear it. You're a valuable member of
the team, and I like working with you.
```

95

This sentiment was at odds with his attitude from yesterday. There was no sign of the threats he'd been making previously, no acknowledgment of them. I was unsure what to make of it.

"Hi," someone said, prompting me to look up from my phone. It was the boy I'd seen before, about my age. He was a little taller than I, with glasses and long dark bangs that fell into them. "What's your name?"

"Emily," I responded. I wondered briefly if I should be using my fake name to make it harder for my parents to find me. Too late now. "Yours?"

"Ezra. This your first day at the shoe?"

I blinked. "The what?"

He smiled. "Here. We call it the shoe. I haven't seen you before."

"Oh. Yeah. I just got here last night. Why do you call it the shoe?"

"S-H-U. Subsidized housing unit. SHU."

"Oh."

"Yeah. So what's your deal? How'd you end up here?"

"I'd rather not talk about it."

Ezra laughed. "You'll fit right in. No one wants to talk about it."

"Well, do you?" I asked.

"Nope." He winked. I wasn't sure what he meant with the wink.

The conversation continued a while longer. He gave me some tips about living in the SHU: which bathrooms were in the best state of repair; what was socially unacceptable to ask the other residents; and where I could get a job for someone my age with no high school diploma (I pretended to be intently interested when he talked about that, while knowing that I'd never

96

use the information). Eventually he left for work (at a coffee shop down the street), and I was left to kill time on my own.

CHAPTER 19

I got to the library just before it opened at 9 a.m. The librarian who unlocked the front doors gave me a bit of an odd look, clearly meant to say 'shouldn't you be in school?', but she didn't challenge me. Immediately, I headed upstairs towards the teens section, where I could start my workday. I claimed my favorite of the PCs in that section: in the back corner, the screen facing towards the walls. It was ideal for anyone who didn't want someone looking over their shoulder. I wasn't really hiding anything, since no one would be able to look at my gameplay and see what we were planning, but sometimes people would just watch you play a video game here. It made me uncomfortable.

No one else was in the section at the moment, though, as it was a school morning. Other teens would be grinding through their second classes of the day, wishing desperately to be out of there.

I grinned. This was the best feeling I'd had since leaving my parents' house. The freedom sank in, overcoming the trepidation that had crushed me.

Logging into *PlanetCrash*, I pulled up the list of items we still needed. Jessica was tracking down the rarest ones, but some of the more common items I could probably find on my own. The Fire Spirit, for instance, was an item that could be applied to any grenade and would double its efficacy. So a fragmentation grenade would have twice as many shards fly out; a flashbang would blind you for twice as long, etc. It also represented the conflict between what the game considered a 'common' item and what was actually common to players. It wasn't difficult to track down Fire Spirits, as they had relatively high drop rates, but those drops could only occur on certain planets: volcanic ones. They usually weren't worth the effort of the travel into such a dangerous locale, although anyone travelling through for other reasons would be sure to pick some up. I decided that I'd collect more than just one. They could prove invaluable in combat later on, and since we'd only need one to activate the exploit, we could burn through any extras.

Next I pulled up the galaxy map, checking for nearby volcanic planets. Luck favored me: there was one just a few light-years away, called Chal-Kogen. I'd be able to make the trip in a reasonable amount of time with my own meager spaceship. (That thought reminded me that I should be looking to upgrade. I couldn't go around in a tin can forever.)

No reason to waste time: the library would be closing again in just twelve hours. I began a prograde burn away from the fueling station where I'd been docked. I could use a quarter of my fuel to accelerate there, which would leave another quarter to stop, then the other half of my tank to return to the fueling station where I'd docked. I didn't want to cut it too close though: I'd use about a fifth each way, which would leave a significant amount of fuel as a reserve. It'd save money on refueling as well, coming only at the cost of time spent in-flight.

I did a few quick calculations to determine what my trip time would be—about ten minutes—then set my fuel burn rate to go through a fifth of my tank in exactly half that time. So I'd start slowing down as soon as I'd reached maximum velocity, with no 'coasting period' at top speed. I could tell the engine to burn the same amount of fuel all at once, but that was less efficient and would end up taking longer for the full flight. Experienced *PlanetCrash* pilots would only use those high-thrust ma-

99

neuvers during combat, when you couldn't spend minutes at a time accelerating up to your desired speed.

I used the remainder of the flight time to pull up the map of Chal-Kogen and look for potential landing sites. Of course, I couldn't land in lava, which ruled out a good two-thirds of the planet right from the start. Beyond that, I wanted to find an area that would have a good difficulty balance: high enough enemy density to maximize the rewards from clearing the area, but low enough not to pose a significant threat to me. Dying out here would almost certainly get me kicked out of the project, unless I pulled a miracle to get back to within reasonable level range before Cubism found out.

Eventually, I determined that the best spot to land seemed to be an island of rock in the southwestern hemisphere of the planet. It met all the conditions I was looking for, plus it had an extremely cool local enemy type: dragons. You didn't get to fight many of those in *PlanetCrash*, but I was a firm believer that dragons made everything cooler. That quality was one of the intangibles of the game. Not everything was about min-maxing your levels, ships, and equipment. Sometimes it was just important to remember how damn *cool* the game world was.

An alarm beeped on my UI, warning me that I was about halfway to my destination. I turned off the main engine, then activated the rotational thrusters. These didn't burn any fuel, but just leaked miniscule amounts of air from the ship to rotate it. It took about ten seconds to turn around, after which I began the slow-down burn, then reset the timer to warn me once I was nearing Chal-Kogen.

Four minutes and forty-seven seconds later, I was in a perfect circular orbit over the planet. I climbed into my landing craft and deployed. It would automatically take me down to the surface and land. I couldn't use an orbital drop here, as we had previously: first, my ship wasn't equipped for it, and second, I

100

wouldn't have anyone to pick me up again if I did. So the lander was my substitute.

It took me down far more gently than a planetcrash would, but came at the cost of wasted time just sitting aboard, waiting. After what felt like an eternity, but was probably only about ninety seconds, the lander touched down on the surface of Chal-Kogen. I leapt out immediately, my plasma rifle raised. As fond as I was of my automatic shotgun, it wasn't the proper choice for this environment. I wouldn't be able to keep the dragons in close range: they could *fly*, after all. I already had my eye on my first quarry, an enormous black dragon, smoke rising from its wings with a dangerous beauty. I let my gaze linger on it for a few seconds, appreciating its majesty. Then I stopped wasting time, aimed my rifle at its head, and squeezed off a few shots.

Being a dragon, this action did little more than piss it off. It shook its head towards the sky and let out an enormous roar, calling its brethren to action. Two more dragons descended from the clouds, circling overhead, and a fourth emerged from the ocean of lava that surrounded us, sending a molten spray high into the air. Still, I wasn't worried. Dragons were designed more for the spectacle than as formidable enemies. With my current gear, it would be hard for them to hurt me at all, and it was nigh impossible for me to take damage unless they got in close. And if they did that, my old friend the autoshotgun was equipped as my secondary weapon. In the meantime, the moving targets would be tough to hit, but excellent practice. I took a few more shots at the dragons circling above, whose predictable patterns made them easiest to target.

The dragon that had risen from the inferno below dove towards me to attack. In a split second, I had switched out my weapon and opened fire, pelting my assailant with dozens of shots. The wild spread of the weapon stopped me from hitting consistent headshots, but this proved to be a blessing in disguise: my shots tore large holes in the dragon's wings, forcing it to the ground. It shrieked with the pain. I felt a momentary rush of guilt before turning on the remaining dragons.

They were confused now, unsure of how to react. Dragons were intelligent enough that they would have learned that diving towards me would not end well for them, but not so far from instinct that they felt able to just abandon their territory. The two overhead circled and continued to fly around one another, as if arguing with each other about what to do.

The third came to a landing beside the one I'd wounded, protecting it. Perhaps they were mates? This made it an easy target, though, and I switched back to my rifle and pounded fire into the dragon: in the head, the wings, the chest, and finally the eyes. It took a great deal of damage before it stopped moving, likely dead.

With one dragon killed and another grounded, I was free to take patient, well-aimed shots at the dragons circling above. Taking inspiration from the first one I'd shot down, I aimed at the wings rather than their heads. The wings were larger, easier targets, and would bring the dragons down to me, where I could slaughter them easily up close.

The dragons' flight paths became more erratic as I tore hole after hole in their wings, making them more difficult to hit. They caught on to my new strategy, though, and realized they could not maintain their circling overhead indefinitely. It was gaining them nothing. Instead, they dove towards me simultaneously, coming from opposite angles so that I could only hit one. These dragons had started their dives lower than the previous dragon, so I only managed to get one shot off after switching to my autoshotgun before they were blasting fire in my face. My shields could take it, though, only losing a few percentage points to the damage. It was less than I expected, which surprised me. It should have been double that…

I realized why a moment later as the ground fell away from my feet. The other dragon had come from behind to grab me with its talons, lifting me into the air, instead of just breathing fire on me. My heart accelerated as I felt threatened for the first time in the fight. If the dragon dumped me into the lava, I'd die. No way around it.

I blasted the dragon's talons with my shotgun, pulverizing its scales. The dragon let go of me, dropping me towards the lava. I'd expected this, though, and was already grabbing onto its legs. Still, not an ideal situation, but at least I now had some semblance of control over the situation. I was suddenly thankful for all those points I'd put into Agility: the game might not have let me get away with this if I hadn't skilled it up so much. Slowly, I began to climb up the dragon's leg towards its torso. It noticed, of course, that I hadn't fallen when it dropped me, so it began trying to throw me off, doing spins and turning sharply through the air. As long as I didn't move at the wrong time, though, I was fine, so I took a deep breath, tried to remain calm, and synchronized my movements with the lulls in the dragon's attempts to shake me.

The process was painstakingly slow and delicate, but I eventually managed to clamber up the dragon's side and onto its back. Another barrel roll nearly shook me off. I only had the spikes on the dragon's back to cling to now, which were small and smooth, making them less than ideal as grips. Still, I managed to hold on, and went back on the attack. I elected to go for the more difficult target first, as I didn't want to bring down the dragon I was atop while we flew over lava. It was difficult to shoot from one moving target to another, even more difficult on dragons than on spaceships, which moved much more predictably. My advantage was that I'd already worn down the oth-

103

er dragon quite a bit. It still took a few dozen well-aimed shots (plus a good number of less well-aimed ones) before that dragon fell from the sky like the two before it. This left just the one I was riding and the puzzle of how to bring it down without killing my character in the fall. I spent a minute considering the problem while clinging to the dragon's back for dear life as it continued trying to shake me off into the ocean of lava below.

Eventually, a fuzzy, half-formed plan began to emerge in my mind. I wasn't sure if it'd work, but it was certainly better than waiting to get thrown from the dragon's back.

I leapt onto the dragon's left wing in an attempt to use my weight to force it to bank back towards land, where I could bring it down without falling into lava. The dragon barely noticed, and didn't change course at all. I, on the other hand, lost my relatively secure perch on the dragon's back to the much more precarious position on the wing. *Well, crap. So much for that plan.* I struggled to regain my original position, fighting against the powerful, smoky wind. At the same time my mind raced to come up with a new plan. I remembered a few minutes before, when I'd shot holes in one of the other dragon's wings, forcing it to lose altitude and come aground. Could I use that to try to control the dragon's flight against its will? It was terribly risky, even more so than my previous plan. There was no way to patch the dragon's wings once I'd shot holes in them, no getting back to where I'd started. This would be permanent.

There was only one way to find out if it would work, though, and no better plans were coming to mind. I re-equipped my shotgun, but turned off automatic firing. Accidentally blowing a hole too large would just cause us to crash into the lava without being able to reach land. I took a deep breath, then pulled the trigger. The dragon roared with pain and we began dropping altitude slowly, but the dragon didn't

104

turn as I'd hoped. This would only work to reduce altitude, not control our position.

A moment later, though, the dragon turned of its own accord, and start heading back towards the island where I'd landed. *What?* I was momentarily confused. Why was the dragon heading back towards land? A possibility occured to me. Could the dragon not swim without its wings? I remembered when one had burst from the lava earlier: it had been pumping its wings incredibly hard as it emerged from the surface, hence the wild spray of lava that had followed its surfacing. Perhaps they were necessary. And if the dragons couldn't breathe without air, landing in lava with damaged wings would be a death sentence for them, same as for me.

As we came overland, I opened fire again, causing our altitude to drop faster and faster as I tore new holes in the dragon's wing. Soon we came crashing down into the island, the force of our impact throwing rock, ash, and soot high into the air. I was thrown from the dragon's back and into the dirt. Another roar came from the dragon, which now stood behind me. I spun around just in time to see it bearing down on me, mouth open wide. I raised my shotgun, flipping it back onto automatic, and opened fire in the same moment as the dragon threw a jet of its firebreath at me. I could no longer see anything beyond my HUD through the smoke and flame, but kept my finger firmly down on the trigger. My shields dropped incredibly quickly and my shotgun was fast overheating between the ambient heat, the firebreath, and the internal energy of my shots. The firebreath ended with my shields at only 12% capacity and a moment later my shotgun stopped firing.

I could now see the damage I'd inflicted upon the dragon during that exchange: there were large patches where I'd ripped its scales off, and its wings were in tatters. It struggled to keep its head aloft, weighed down by wounds along its neck. I dropped

105

my overheated shotgun and equipped my pulse rifle. Once a weapon overheated, it was permanently useless. The shotgun had served me well since I'd acquired it, but its time was up. Besides, a quick check of my exp showed that I'd level up to 11 once I'd finished off the dragons.

Overcome with exhaustion, the dragon before me was no longer able to put up a fight, and barely resisted as I put it out of its misery with a few pulse rifle shots in each eye. I trudged back over to the other three dragons, which were too wounded to move but not yet dead, and finished them off similarly. It was almost painful to destroy such beautiful creatures, and I forced myself to recall that it was just a game.

As expected, I levelled up from the kills, closing some of the gap between me and the rest of the team. This left me with a tricky decision. The points I'd been putting in Agility so far had paid off massively just now, allowing me to survive as the dragon had attempted to throw me off its back. That meant, however, that I already had enough Agi to pull of crazy moves like that, and the two points I gained each level would be better suited somewhere else. Ultimately, I decided to put one each into Strength and Precision. Agility was high enough for now that I was probably into diminishing returns—it was time to let the other stats catch up a bit.

Now it was time to loot. *Let's see what these dragons have in their hoards.*

It was a good haul, all told. The four dragons I'd killed had no fewer than *fifteen* Fire Spirits between them. I'd hold on to two for the glitch (we only needed one, but it never hurt to have a spare), and would keep the other thirteen for use in combat. There were a few other interesting items including Dragon ichor, scales, and teeth. All of these were useful in the hands of a skilled ship craftsman. On top of everything else, there was a good amount of EC and "wares," items that had no

106

value in combat and weren't worth anything except to sell to NPC merchants.

Looking through my inventory, I realized I'd built up a good amount of EC and wares that I hadn't yet sold, and decided I should go on a bit of a shopping spree to upgrade my gear. Before that, though, I needed to get off-planet, for safety.

I returned to my lander and instructed the autopilot to take me back up to my ship. Once the lander automatically docked, I jumped into my cockpit and ordered a repeat of my previous flightplan. I was pointed in the opposite direction from my original flight, so the same thruster burns would put me exactly back where I'd started.

I paused to check the time IRL as I pulled into the fueling station. It was just past 9:30 a.m., still too early to call up Jeremy. Time for my shopping spree, then. The marketplace of *PlanetCrash* wasn't a physical place (well, none of *PlanetCrash* was a *physical* place), but rather was on the in-game version of the internet. NPC vendors sold many common items and players could put to market anything they didn't want. Whatever you bought would just appear in your inventory and anything you listed for sale would be removed from your inventory until you pulled the listing. So far, I'd relied entirely on loot for this character, but with the passing of my autoshotgun, it was time to see what was available.

After refueling, which didn't take up a significant amount, I was left with just over 17 million EC, plus a couple million more worth of unsold wares, which I listed on the market. It sounded like a lot more than it was: *PlanetCrash* had a highly inflated currency, because the developers knew that there was this intangible sense of satisfaction that came with having big numbers next to your name in video games. Seeing 17 million EC made me feel rich, even though I couldn't get *that* much for it in game, and nothing for it in real life. That said, I knew it

107

was but a shell of the feeling I'd get at the end of this, when I became *actually* rich...

The first thing to buy was a new ship. My current one was *unbelievably* crappy and being able to get around the galaxy faster and more cheaply would pay dividends throughout all of my solo work.

PlanetCrash had a powerful ship designing and building mechanic, but I'd never been good at it. Besides that, I didn't have the points in Manufacturing to do undertake really cool builds or upgrades. I was sure, though, that Publius was in it all the time, working out small optimizations for our team's vessels. What this meant for me at the moment was that the market-place had hundreds of options of ships for sale, even though the server was only a few days old. There was a significant group of players in the game who played it entirely to create a transporta-tion empire: they'd buy up parts and materials from the market-place, assemble them into custom-designed, high-quality space-craft, then sell them at a premium. If you started doing this early enough, you could gain a reputation on your server, then start getting *employees* who designed ships for you. For a few play-ers, this would spiral into large corporations, which would form into powerful factions on the political stage of the server: with-out a trade agreement with a powerful shipbuilding faction, you'd never be able to field as many high-quality ships into a battle as an opponent who did have a deal.

While I appreciated that all this existed, I found it mind-numbingly boring. Who went into *PlanetCrash* just to design ships for a *boss* all day? How was that an escape from the real world? I didn't get it.

Regardless, the server was still young enough that no one was particularly well-established. It was an unwritten rule of this sector of the game that you should never advertise yourself based on accomplishments in a previous server and it was enforced by a quiet shunning of anyone who attempted to create a trans-server brand. This was a striking contrast to many of the other main factions, like the Legion of Honor, which would exist in the exact same form in every server, always doing their best to recruit as many as they could. The problem with this blatant attempt to gain immediate influence over a server was that it didn't create any loyalty. I thought back to my previous character, Gart Gasper. As soon as he'd died, I'd abandoned the faction he'd been with, The Jovian Moon. They didn't actually care about me and I knew it. I was just a pawn in their game. It was fun to be that for a while, especially when they geared me up with free, good equipment before difficult missions, which always gave me a rush, but the bond was just surface level. I hadn't even considered rejoining them when I'd logged onto NA-22 for the first time. Good thing too, or I might not have found Cubism's posting.

I applied a filter onto the list of ships for sale, so that it would only show me the ones costing about 10 million EC. This seemed like the appropriate amount to spend. Since ships were the only commodity in *PlanetCrash* that had custom variants, their price was much larger than weapons or armor, which just got slapped onto the market by anyone who wasn't happy with their loot drops. Still, I wanted to keep enough left over to get some really good stuff to equip myself with, even after the ship.

Adding another filter, I limited my search to subcapital ships. Players in *PlanetCrash* categorized ships into four main groups: fighters, subcapitals, capitals, and megacruisers. Fighters were specialized ships that were small, only large enough to hold a single pilot, with no passengers or storage, but they were fast, and had surprisingly powerful weapons. You usually only saw them as parts of a large fleet, as they didn't have very good independent range and had to dock with larger ships. They were also expensive, given the need for high-power, lightweight engines and weapons to allow for great combat potential without sacrificing speed or maneuverability.

Capital ships were the main backbones of any major fleet in the galaxy. They covered a wide range of ships, including transports, artillery ships, frigates, cruisers, destroyers, and corvettes. Each of these subclasses had a specific, well-defined role in a fleet battle group. Corvettes were the smallest of capital ships, barely bigger than the subcapitals, but much more heavily armed and armored. Like fighters, these had to have expensive weapons and motors to maintain their speed in combat, so they could end up costing more than ten times what subcapitals tended to. Some even included stealth systems. Given their small size and high speed compared to the other capital ships, corvettes tended to be used for scouting in a major battle. They were small enough that most of the enemy capital ships wouldn't prefer them over other targets, but strong enough to fight off a decent amount of fighters. This typically led to a sub-battle inside every major space battle, exclusively between the corvettes, jockeying for positioning and information inside the larger battle.

Artillery ships devoted almost all of their mass to a single giant gun. They were devastatingly powerful when they connected a shot, but were slow and poorly armored, meaning they could be sitting ducks for any enemy corvettes that decided they'd done enough scouting for the day. Usually, you'd have to leave some defenses behind to keep the artillery in play. Artillery went in and out of fashion among the commanders of large fleets, who often preferred to invest in high-mobility fleets over the slower and heavier fleets that artillery ships would fit into more easily. No one in this server yet had amassed a large enough fleet for the paradigm to be well defined yet, but on NA-21, it had been all about maneuverability, so artillery ships were overlooked.

110

Transports did exactly what it said on the tin: most of their volume was devoted to space to carry troops and supplies between planets. If you wanted to mount an invasion of another faction's planet, you'd need these in spades. They were heavily armored as they tended to be targets for enemy fire, and they only had a few weapons, designed to ward off enemy fighters rather than engage capital ships.

Destroyers had anti-stealth systems, good maneuverability, and 'catch', which referred to the ability to slow down and even stop enemy ships against their will. Boarding parties would usually deploy from a destroyer after the target ship had been incapacitated, but not destroyed, meaning the title was a bit of a misnomer.

Frigates were a bit larger and slower than destroyers and were the primary escort craft of a fleet. Any transports would be guarded by frigates, as would artillery (if the commanders favored those ships). They had a mix of both lighter, anti-fighter weapons and heavier, anti-capital ones. They were highly versatile and you'd see them all over any space battle in about ten different roles.

Cruisers were the largest of the capital ships and packed a serious punch. Funnily enough, though, they were confined to only small and mid-sized space battles, battles between unimportant factions or minor engagements in a large conflict. In any major battle, they'd be overshadowed by their big sister that did the same job: the dreadnought.

Dreadnoughts were one of the two types of megacruisers. They weren't very maneuverable, but they were weapons of mass destruction, capable of single-handedly fighting several capital ships at once. They were the instant focal point of any battle that they were in. A single dreadnought cost trillions of EC at the minimum, so only the largest of empires in a server could afford them. A battle without a dreadnought would al-

111

most invariably consist of the fleet that lacked that power fleeing and a battle with multiple dreadnoughts could change the political landscape of the galaxy dramatically if they were brought down, as they represented a significant portion of the resources and combat potential of any faction.

The other type of megacruiser were carriers. They were similar in size to dreadnoughts, but lacked the same armor or armament. Once they'd deployed their hundreds of fighters at the beginning of a battle, there wasn't much point in targeting them, and adding weapons would only make them more attractive for enemy commanders, threatening the investment that a faction had put in such a large ship. They largely went unrecognized, though the fighters they carried could turn the tide of a battle in the right circumstances.

Finally, there were the subcapitals, which I was looking at. These were small ships, designed to only hold one or two passengers, plus a little storage, but still able to traverse far longer distances than fighters were. This came at the cost of combat power: if someone started shooting at my current ship, I'd have no choice but to flee. There were a huge variety of subcapitals, with some focused on stealth, like the one I'd used as Gart Gasper, some on speed, some on range, and others on freight capacity. In my case, it was probably best to get a good balance of speed and range, as I didn't expect the other factors to come up much: I wasn't our primary pilot and the ship would only be for personal use, ferrying me between my independent projects.

I perused my various options. There were some devilishly stylish ships, but at this point in my character progression I wasn't willing to pay a premium to fly around in something that looked cool, tempting as that was. I eventually settled on a fast but inexpensive ship (which I named the *Venture*), at the lower end of my price range, but still able to make the trip I'd done earlier this morning in about three-quarters of the time it had

112

taken me. Besides which, its range was far greater, enough to make it between any two refueling stations. I'd never have to get on another commercial flight like the one that had led to me killing Val. The tradeoff I was making to save money was on its armament, which there wasn't much of. That said, I doubted I'd get into a dogfight in this subcapital, as long as I was careful where I flew. Ship to ship combat would more likely happen when I was aboard Publius' craft. I finalized the deal, dropping eight and a half million EC, fully half my wealth, for the upgrade.

Time to see what sorts of fun things I could get with the other half of my EC.

I'd been levelling my original pulse rifle up to as I went, which was why it was still useful this whole time, but it didn't have any special bonuses to distinguish it. Now was the time to find a replacement, probably a rare pulse rifle at my current level. I set filters on the market to help my search: rarity set to everything above common (epics and legendaries would be more expensive, but depending on their attributes might be worth it), and gave a level range of twenty-three to twenty-five: my own level was twenty-four, so this was a bit of a give or take. Ideally I'd find a level twenty-four, as otherwise I'd have to work to get a twenty-three up to a twenty-four, and a twenty-five would have penalties associated with it until I hit that level myself, but only one level of difference in either direction wouldn't be too bad.

Scrolling through the marketplace, I noticed how, as usual, many of the rares were absolute crap, worse even than the default rifle that I was retiring. This was the downside of owning randomly generated loot in the game: there was no guarantee that it'd be any good. Rares, especially randomly generated ones, tended to come with one advantage and one disadvantage as compared to the default items. Some of the developer's hand-designed rares wouldn't have any drawbacks, but that was the exception rather than the rule. This design strategy was a good way to ensure that most rare items were interesting variations on the base items, without becoming horribly "OP," or overpowered. The downside was, of course, that many of the items just plain sucked. I had to wade through dozens, hundreds, of these items to find a handful of good ones.

I came up with a shortlist of a few items that seemed like solid upgrades, worth the prices that were being asked for them, and eventually settled on a pulse rifle that had an attached grappling hook. This decision was prompted by the experience of having been spaced a few days ago: I didn't want to have to use the delicate maneuver of shooting behind me for thrust again and a grappling hook would make recovery in that situation much more robust. Beyond which, the enhanced mobility would come in handy for on-planet combat situations. It was one of the developer custom items, as its grappling hook had probably required special programming, so didn't have any associated drawbacks. All in all, I thought it was a great pickup, even though it did set me back another million EC.

On top of the grappling gun (as I'd mentally named it), I picked up another automatic shotgun to replace the one I'd ruined on Chal-Kogen. At 26, it was slightly above my current level, which meant I wouldn't be able to use it immediately, but these were rare items: there was only one on the entire market and the coincidence of having it close to my level, if not exact, was too good to pass up. I didn't expect it'd last long on the market if I hadn't bought it, and it could be weeks before someone again listed one in my range. With another three million EC spent on that, I decided to call my shopping spree a success and move on.

114

Checking the IRL time again told me it was just past 10 a.m. Time to call Jeremy. He answered my Discord call almost immediately, but sounded groggy.

"Know, Em, when I said 'don't call before ten' I didn't expect you to call me *exactly at* ten."

I smiled. "It's not exactly ten: it's ten-o-three!" I replied brightly. "You've had a hundred and eighty seconds!"

"You still woke me up," he muttered.

"C'mon, get in game," I said, brushing off his sleepiness. "My clock's ticking: library closes in eleven hours."

That seemed to wake him up a bit. "You're playing at the library? So you did figure it out…"

"Yeah. I ran away last night." It was strange to say aloud; the way the words tasted in my mouth was unexpected, tinged with equal parts contrasting freedom and apprehension.

"Where are you staying? I'm guessing you don't have a secret studio apartment on Newbury street?"

"I wish. No, I'm at a SHU near the Southie-Dot area."

"Andrew Square?"

"That's the one. You know it?"

"Course I know it," he replied, sounding a bit more awake now. "I live over on Telegraph Hill. You should stop by sometime."

I couldn't tell if he was joking, and didn't know how to respond regardless, so I went back to the more immediate matter. "I'm gonna be able to be online a lot more now, obviously, so I think we might want to enter a duel league together."

Duel leagues were most commonly used as a way for marines seeking promotion in one of the larger factions to prove themselves, but they were also a great source of exp and EC if you could win. They worked in a similar way to the practice

115

battles we'd done on Almanac, but were far more exciting and rewarding to participate in.

Four duelists in two teams would be dropped into a randomized arena and fight to the death. But unlike the Almanac practice battles, levels and equipment would be equalized beforehand. They were purely tests of skill. The tournament software would track the stats of every team, ranking everyone. Every month, the leaderboard would reset, everyone's rank would be eliminated, and the system would distribute exp and EC to all of the participants according to their final placing on the leaderboard, number of matches played, and current level. Your level was taken into account to normalize the exp handout and to account for the fact that it took a lot more exp to get from level twenty to twenty-one than it did to get from level one to level two.

There were downsides, of course. You didn't get the exp immediately, and if you didn't place very well in the final standings then it was a highly inefficient way of levelling up. But if you had the time and the skill to put in a lot of battles and top the leaderboard, it could be both faster and safer than levelling in live combat.

"Ohh, now that's a fun idea!" Even though I'd never seen his face, I could imagine Jeremy's wicked grin at that moment. He seemed like a guy with a competitive streak and while everyone likes making money, our group strategy probably wasn't satisfying his desire to *win* at something. That was the most powerful feeling: knowing that you'd won not because your character was better, but because *you* were better.

"Let me pull up the list of leagues," I replied, taking Jeremy's response as an affirmative. Finding the right league was a miniature challenge in itself. Join one too old and you'd never have the time to catch up on the leaderboards to the people who'd been in from the start, but join too early (or start your

116

own!) and you'd have a hard time finding matches. We wanted lots of matches, and quickly, so that probably meant a league that was in its adolescence. The best way to find these ones would not have been to sort by league age, but by growth rate. Unfortunately, that wasn't an option the *PlanetCrash* developers gave you.

I minimized out of the game, pulling up archived versions of the *PlanetCrash* leagues list from the game's official website for yesterday at this time, then a second tab on the browser with today's data. The number of players was a reported statistic in both cases and some quick subtraction showed me that the fastest growing league over the past day had been one sponsored and set up by the Legion of Honor. Apparently, the first place winners would be entitled to high-ranking positions as field officers within the Legion, although Jeremy and I would obviously have to decline that particular reward. Other than that, though, this league seemed perfect, so I signed us up.

Just as I'd hoped, hardly five minutes after Jeremy logged into *PlanetCrash*, we got thrown into our first match. It was an interesting one, too: a 'battle royale.' The more advanced leagues would use these custom matches when enough people were searching for a fight at once. Instead of breaking us off into pairs of 2v2 teams, the game threw a hundred participants into a large arena with only one rule: last one alive would win. *PlanetCrash*'s Battle Royale system lacked some of the features that a dedicated BR game would have included: notably looting and dropping into the map. We simply spawned fully equipped at a randomized location. I'd always thought it was strange, given that loot was already in the game and that *PlanetCrash*'s titular mechanic was the ability to drop onto any planet. Perhaps the devs had simply decided to try to differentiate themselves in this way. It had worked though: instead of the frantic looting that dominated most BRs, *PlanetCrash*'s mode was all about the hunt.

117

As soon as we spawned, I glanced around at our surroundings to get my bearings. There was only one Battle Royale map in *PlanetCrash* and I'd played enough matches to know it better than I knew the streets in Back Bay.

There were four "biomes," each with a dramatically different look, which made it especially easy to get a quick idea of your approximate location. We'd spawned into the tundra quarter, but not near any structures or towns. Instead, we were in a valley between a group of snow-dusted hills. Having the low ground meant we were unlikely to be spotted, but would be at a major disadvantage if anyone did happen to engage us from the summit of any of the hills.

A short ways to the south, the terrain would fade from tundra into a dense evergreen forest: the second biome of the map and my personal favorite. To the west, the tundra transitioned aggressively and unrealistically into a grassland biome, with grass tall enough to conceal anyone who bothered to crouch down. There was little other cover, save for the grass and a few small towns, so firefights there could get deadly fast. To the southeast, a desert biome filled the remaining quarter of the map with dunes and oases.

In the center stood The Mountain. From its summit you could see practically the entire map and it was near impossible to sneak up on someone based there. That made it by far the most contested piece of real estate and tended to force bloodbaths on the slopes and paths leading up to the summit.

Since everyone spawned fully equipped, there was no need for the devs to delay in pushing us all towards the center. An orbital bombardment of the fringes of the map began immediately and slowly, steadily pushing everyone towards the Mountain. While the final safe area was randomized, the summit of the Mountain would always be inside it, making that ground even more prized. Personally, I hated taking the summit. It was too obvious. Everyone who wasn't there was prepared for someone who was. It left no chance to take your foes by surprise.

"You wanna head south?" I asked Jeremy.

"Let's do it." He didn't seem to have particularly strong feelings one way or the other. I took the lead through the valleys towards the forests.

As we ventured south the tundra hills gradually flattened out and began to host the occasional tree. It was here, on the border between the biomes, that Jeremy spotted footprints in the snow. In line with our destination, they showed a southbound path into the woods.

"Wanna try to chase these kids down?" he said, gesturing at the trail.

I raised an eyebrow. It took a second to remember that he couldn't actually see me. "Who says they're kids?" I replied, asking aloud the question I'd tried to express facially.

"Does it matter?" Jeremy said. "We can kill adults just as easily."

"Then hell yeah, let's get 'em."

With that, we took off again, dashing along the path our quarries had left behind. I did my best to keep one eye on the ground and the other scanning our surroundings. It was easy to follow the trail in the snow, but once we hit the forest, the clear footprints would fade as the snow grew thinner and eventually disappeared. Without snow on the ground, tracking grew more difficult but it was still far from impossible.

Jeremy paused as the snow ended and we reached the last footprint in sight. "I haven't done much woodland tracking before," he said. "Can you watch the ground? I'll keep you covered."

I nodded in response, this time remembering to command my avatar to mimic the motion simultaneously.

The increased effort I had to put into following the trail from that point slowed down our pace through the forest and before long, the bombardment ring had closed in sufficiently that we were forced to abandon our pursuit and simply head east towards The Mountain. It was a frustrating turn of events, an annoying downside of the design decisions that the developers had made.

As luck would have it, though, we found ourselves a short ways behind another duo as they fled the closing ring of destruction. Were they the ones we'd been following? Possible, but there was no way to tell for sure.

"Ahead, two o'clock!" I called out to Jeremy, even though a blind fish would have been able to see them by now.

"Got it. Let's take them out." Your life always sat on a knife's edge in *PlanetCrash* BR, where everyone was equipped with a weapon that could kill in just two headshots. If someone got behind you without you knowing, you were as good as dead.

"I got the one on the left. Ready to shoot when you are." Jeremy nodded his assent a moment later, and I started a countdown. "Three, two, one, fire!"

Our shots were simultaneous, and each perfectly on its mark. But, just as I'd fired, my target had stepped to the side to avoid a bush that I could now see was in his way. My burst grazed by him, not close enough to kill, just dropping his shields, with a distinctive blue flash as they broke.

He reacted with incredible speed, dropping to the ground before I adjusted by aim and fired off my second burst, which flew clean over his head. He was out of sight now, having rolled into the bushes that he'd sidestepped originally. I cursed, tried to equip a grenade, then cursed again when I remembered that

120

PlanetCrash BR didn't have those. My heart rate accelerated to a blast beat.

"You *missed?*" Jeremy cried indignantly. His target was smoking on the ground, which gave him some right to complain, but I still didn't appreciate it.

"Shut up and flank right," I said tersely, dashing off to the left before he had a chance to respond. A quick glance back showed that he'd complied. While I checked that though, our quarry let loose a barrage of return fire from his position. No direct hits, thank God, but two ricochets and a flurry of splinters that took my shields down below half. I ducked into cover behind a tree, paranoid since I hadn't seen exactly where the shots had come from. Another round of fire came as I cowered, smashing bits of the tree into flaming chips and bark. I dove even lower to the ground, hoping to avoid the shots. I was only partially successful, and the remainder of my shielding was now fried.

"Are you behind this guy yet?" I snapped at Jeremy.

"I think so...I'll try to draw him my way."

With that, Jeremy stopped running and sent his own burst of fire back at where he'd seen the hostile shoot from.

A moment of stillness followed, then another.

"I think I got him," Jeremy said.

Releasing the breath I hadn't realized I'd been holding, I stood back up.

"Thanks. He nearly had me there."

I could hear the smile in Jeremy's reply. "I got your back, don't worry, don't panic."

The ring was probably closing in on us again, so I turned to check its progress. Still a good ways out, but we shouldn't dawdle much longer...

Gunfire erupted behind me, and I spun back around just in time to see two laser blasts hit Jeremy in the back of the head. He dropped like a stone. The player we'd been hunting had been playing dead: and now he'd taken out Jeremy. He spun on me as I frantically raised my weapon on him, but he was the faster on the trigger. A moment later my screen went black.

`You placed 28th out of 50 teams. Spectate/Quit`

I disconnected from the match, frustrated. Jeremy sighed on the other end of the call, obviously feeling the same way. We stewed in silence for a few seconds, but I knew there was only one thing to do.

"Ready for another?" I asked.

Our next two matches weren't battle royales, but relatively easy duels against inexperienced opposition. After those, though, we came up against the Legion of Honor's Champions in the tournament: a pair of fighters tasked with representing the Legion and entrusted by them to win the tournament. They were much more difficult than the kids we'd just taken out.

It was a terrain-ban style duel. Instead of totally randomizing the environment that we'd fight in, the game would generate three possibilities. One team would ban one of the three, preventing it from being played, and the other would choose which of the remaining two they wanted to fight on.

Since they won a virtual coin toss, the Legion's Champions had the ban, and we had the pick. The first environment was a curious one: a submerged cave. I'd fought in those a couple times, they tended to be rife with underwater passageways around the main land areas. It was a flanker's paradise. Second was a set of ruined buildings on a hill. Pretty standard, but not overly exciting. The third was a wooded area, not unlike the one we'd died in during our battle royale. I was pleased to see

122

that this was the Champions' choice of ban, as I hadn't wanted to go back.

"The LCs are probably pretty practiced on the ruins," Jeremy pointed out. "It's one of the most common terrains."

"You want to do the cave?" I asked, to confirm that was what he was getting at.

"Hell yeah. It'll confuse them as much as it does us."

I wasn't sure that I liked that way of thinking about it, but I punched it in as our selection anyway. The world faded to black as the game world began to load in.

The blacks melded into oranges as the cave appeared around us, lit solely by torchlight. A bit rustic, given the sci-fi setting, but still a good aesthetic.

Two dark tunnels were ahead of us, and a deep pool of water behind. No doubt it'd connect up somewhere else.

"Which way?" Jeremy asked as the countdown timer to the match began.

"Let's stick together. Should we try the pool, or is that too risky?"

He chuckled. "It'll be fun, if nothing else."

The countdown reached zero.

"Commence Match."

I dove into the pool, with Jeremy just behind me. It was near pitch black, as the torchlight couldn't penetrate far under the water. A light flicked on behind me: apparently Jeremy had a flashlight equipped.

I felt momentarily foolish: obviously the underwater cave would be dark. I should have realized that before proposing diving. Too late now.

Jeremy must have noticed that I didn't have a light and swam ahead of me, taking the lead. We were in a small tunnel—which would have been extremely claustrophobic in real

123

life—that was leading deeper into the cave. There was only one way forward. I followed behind him after getting my bearings, keeping a constant eye on my slowly waning oxygen level.

As we swam forward, the tunnel opened up into a larger lake which connected several other tunnels. I assumed it must have been the main underwater nexus of the map we were playing. Ahead in one of the other tunnels, there was a faint glow. The LCs?

"Kill your flashlight!" I hissed to Jeremy, while simultaneously equipping and raising my rifle.

He obeyed before I even finished speaking. He must have come to the same conclusion: the LCs were approaching. Our natural buoyancy in the game physics pushed us upward towards the surface as we kept our rifles trained on the light ahead, which steadily grew stronger. How had we gotten so far ahead of the LCs?

A glance above told me that I was about to break the surface of the water, so I unequipped my rifle and swam back down. Jeremy hadn't noticed: he'd been watching the approaching light with all his attention. His head emerged from the lake above me, and a barrage of gunfire from the shore killed him before he'd had time to react. *Crap!*

I clung to the rock bottom of the lake, trying to stay still and hidden while I thought. Had the LCs split up, or was the light in the tunnel ahead some kind of automatic diversion? I had no idea how they would have automated that. Was it possible to build autonomous submarines with enough skill points in Manufacturing? I silently cursed myself for having ignored that half of the game. This wasn't the first time it had come back to bite me.

Trying to keep myself pressed to the bottom of the lake, I slowly swam closer to the light until I was directly underneath it. Sure enough, it wasn't a player at all but a miniature robotic

124

boat with a flashlight on the front. I didn't have much time to ponder this, though, as my oxygen was starting to run low.

Fortunately, the light from the robot was just enough for me to make out the tunnels out of here. Which one would the LCs not be watching? They had at least one person on the surface, keeping an eye on the lake and probably the tunnels towards our spawn point. Where would the other be?

Well, one of them had to have put the robot into the water, right? I swam towards the tunnel that it had come from. Hopefully I could catch out one of the LCs alone, which would put me in a 1v1 with the other. That I could handle, probably. Hopefully.

The light from the robot didn't penetrate very far, so once I was in the tunnel the world was once again pitch black. The tunnel we'd come into the lake from had been relatively straight, though, so I hoped that just swimming forward would get me to an exit. If not, well…I took another glance at my oxygen levels. Not long left before I'd start to drown.

Sure enough, though, the torchlight from another exit was coming into view. And a shadow was cast from it: one of the LCs was standing guard over the exit. I again pressed myself to the rock, creeping forward and hoping not to be seen. Once the LC's head was in view, I re-equipped my rifle and fired. Water boiled around each laser burst as they streaked out of the pool and into the LC's helmet. It took only a few shots before he went down. I scrambled to get out of the water: my oxygen was just about spent, and I wanted to be able to take a defensive position on land in case the other LC was rushing me.

Once back on dry land, I knelt behind a rock and aimed my rifle towards the passage back to the lake, lamenting the loss of my auto-shotgun on Chal-Kogen. It would have been invaluable in these confines and I hadn't yet leveled high enough to use my new one.

Footsteps echoed behind me. Was there another passage? I dove over the rock I'd been crouching behind, levelling my rifle at...nothing. All that was behind me was a wall of rock. *What?* I thought for sure I'd heard footsteps...

Then I saw...another robot, much smaller, sitting low to the ground with a speaker pointed towards me. Damn, these guys were good.

I spun around again, just in time to be shot in the face.

"Match complete."

Frustrated by another loss, I bade Jeremy a terse farewell before disconnecting from PlanetCrash and heading home.

CHAPTER 20

I made it back to the SHU around 9:30 that evening, just in time to catch their free dinner, which ended at 10. I'd have to keep that in mind going forward: no dallying at or around the library after close, or I'd miss one of my two daily meals. The growling of my stomach from skipping lunch (a daily phenomenon to which I was doomed in order to get my *PlanetCrash* hours in) was a stark reminder that missing even one or two trains back from the library would mean going almost twenty-four hours without any food. It wasn't a pleasant thought.

Ezra was about to leave the dining hall as I entered, but stopped himself as he saw me coming in, sitting back down at one of the tables to the side and gesturing for me to join him.

After acknowledging him, I went to grab my food then sat at his table.

"How was work?" I asked. Small talk had never been my strong suit, but it seemed like a safe enough question, unlikely to spiral out of control.

He laughed in response, his dark eyes glimmering behind long black bangs. "Awful, as usual. Twelve hours of pretentious upper-middle class a-holes who think they're 'authentic Italians' for drinking espresso but who don't know that a macchiato isn't the upside-down latte that Starbucks likes to pretend it is."

I wasn't sure what to make of this. He'd said his day was awful and had just gone on a rant, but the whole time he'd seemed upbeat, almost chipper even. As if he enjoyed hating his job?

Ezra didn't give me a chance to respond, though. "You were out all day as well, I see, what with your arrival here so late. Doing a door-to-door, pavement-hitting job hunt? I appreciate the effort friend, but that just ain't how you get hired this century."

"I was at the library."

"Ahhhh, see, that's it, that's what it's about: online applications. That's all it is these days, you've got it." He paused for a moment. "Unless you were doing something else: studying for your GED?"

I nodded, then shook my head. "Something else yes, GED no."

Ezra raised his eyebrows. "Do tell."

I hesitated. What would he think of the truth: that I'd been playing *PlanetCrash* for twelve hours? His expectation seemed to be that I'd be doing all I could to get back on my feet and move out and I doubted this would qualify in his mind. I certainly didn't want to tell him about the heist plan, in case he was a snitch.

I told him anyway. Not about the heist, which was too risky to advertise, but I didn't want to lie.

He flipped. "Are you serious? Why the hell are you wasting your time with that crap?"

Not knowing how to respond, I just sat in silence, gaze fixed down on my food.

"I can't believe this!" he continued. "You're not even trying to make things better for yourself are you?"

He gave me another chance to respond, but I still didn't know what to say.

"Oh God," he said, genuine horror encroaching into his features. "Don't tell me you ran away from your parents so that you could just play more video games? What, do you think you're going to become a professional gamer someday? Is that all you want?"

My silence was the only confirmation he needed. He stood up and began to walk away, but turned around to give one final comment. "You know, it's not too late to turn back. You can still fix this. Just go home. Or don't. Ruin your life if you want. I don't care."

He left the dining area.

I was crushed. Logically, I knew that he had good reasons for thinking and saying what he did, that he couldn't see the whole picture like I could. Beyond which, I'd only met him yesterday, what did I care what he thought? I knew the answer to that, though: I cared what he thought because he was my only chance for a real-life friend in this place, until my payday came and I got out.

I took another bite of my food, which seemed to change to ash in my mouth. All of the euphoria of today's progress with Jeremy was overpowered by only a few minutes' talk with Ezra. It was disheartening, terrifying even, how quickly he'd been driven away. The dedication that Cubism demanded of me had taken so much from me so quickly. My home, my security, and even my ability to have positive interactions with those outside of the project: all of these had fallen apart.

Ezra's reaction brought uncomfortable questions to my mind. Had I made the right decision? Was the possibility of living my dream worth the risk of the collapse of my stable, if disappointing life? Should I have been content to work a 9 to 5 that I hated, living for the evenings and weekends?

I didn't know the answers. It was too late, anyway: I'd committed to this. That thought didn't help me sleep, though.

CHAPTER 21

I caught up with Cubism the next morning when he called me on Discord, shortly after I'd arrived at the library.

"Morning, Emily!" He sounded bright and chipper, a stark difference from the last time we'd talked.

"Morning," I replied, still sleepy.

"I wanted to talk, if you've got a couple minutes?"

"Go ahead."

"Great...first of all, I want to say that I'm really glad you're committing to us. Jeremy told me you two put in a lot of good hours yesterday and if you're able to keep that up consistently, you'll be a huge asset."

"Thanks..." I wasn't sure where he was going with this.

"That said, I also want to apologize. I was deeply, inappropriately harsh on you when we last spoke. I do stand by the substance of what I said; I do need your full commitment, but I could have and should have said it in a far more calm and respectful way...I'm really relying on this project to work out, and I'm super stressed about it, but I took that out on you which was unfair."

"It's okay," I replied, even though I wasn't sure that it was. I did sympathize with his stress, though: if he'd put himself in as fragile a position as I had, it made perfect sense why he was so tyrannical about who could remain on the team. As much as I'd liked Val, standing where I did today rather than where I had then, I was glad she was gone. Towing someone along would not be a good use of our time, energy, or resources. We had to press forward.

"I'm sure you've put a lot on the line in your life to continue with us and I really, sincerely appreciate that. I didn't have the choice to do that, it was thrust upon me, and I highly regard you for coming to this as a decision on your own, without the pressures that are on me."

"Thanks." I paused. I'd taken the time to get to know Val and Jeremy better; I probably should with Cubism as well. "So what *are* the pressures that are on you? Are you comfortable sharing?"

He sighed, long and soft. "My dad...my dad has leukemia. He's an immigrant, not a citizen like I am, so he isn't entitled to the free treatments, and we can't afford to pay for them privately. I didn't know how else to raise the money. I considered classic armed robbery, but I knew I wouldn't be able to get enough in a single score to pay for the treatment, so I had to look for a way to up the ante." He chuckled quietly, sadly. "My dad always said knowing so much about this game was a waste of time. Now it might be what saves his life."

"Oh man...I'm so sorry." I wanted to say something more, something useful, something comforting, anything even, but emotional intelligence was never my strong suit. I had no idea where to even begin. I gave it my best effort, though: "We'll make this work. We'll save your dad."

"Thanks," Cubism responded. We sat in silence for a while, but it didn't feel as heavy a silence as it could have. It was, really, the first time I'd ever felt any kind of warmth towards Cubism. In my head he'd been the fearless leader at first, then the harsh dictator. I'd respected him throughout those transitions, but I'd never actually cared about him.

131

It all made sense now, though. I'd considered earlier that he might have put himself in a fragile place, like I had, but I'd never considered that he might have so much more than I did riding on the outcome of our operation. He needed this to succeed, and to succeed relatively quickly, or his life might well be torn apart.

Eventually, Cubism re-broke the silence. "I'd almost forgotten why I asked you to talk in the first place," he began. "It wasn't just to apologize to you. Jessica has located a copy of one of the legendary items, but it's not going to be easy to get."

I snapped back into marine mode. This was much more comfortable territory for me. "What's the situation?"

"One of the larger factions, The Unreals, has a bunker filled with goodies. You got your map open?"

"I do now. In space or on a planet?"

"Planet. Nepthnar."

"Got it." I pulled it up on the galaxy map. "Do we have the coordinates of the bunker?"

"Indeed we do. Forty-two point four five three four degrees north, seventy-six point four seven three five degrees west."

Longitude and latitude were great for *PlanetCrash*: using angles rather than distances allowed a single measurement system to be easily applied to every single planet in the galaxy.

My map automatically zoomed to the point as I entered the figures, giving me an aerial view of the bunker we'd be trying to hit.

"I see it."

"Great. Right now, I just want a feasibility assessment. Do we have any hope of making it into and out of that bunker alive?"

"Give me a second to think."

132

You couldn't tell everything about a location from above, just the general outline of the shapes, which was severely annoying for when you were trying to plan a raid. It was impossible to know, for instance, how many guards there would be in the facility, if there were any at all. It could have a full battalion, or it could be empty, relying on stealth for security. I guessed it wouldn't be the latter, though, because if it was they were doing a terrible job. A stealth bunker you'd at least try to make blend in with the environment and if it held something really important you'd shell out the billions of extra EC to put it entirely underground. Nor was it likely to have a battalion, though. Facilities like that would usually be inside a larger compound, with barracks and practice ranges for the staff that were stationed there. We saw neither, which likely meant that there'd be a limited number of guards on staff there.

Guards weren't the only issue, though. Response time was the next big one. This couldn't be an incredibly quick and dirty job, as we were looking for a specific item. If we were still looking around for it when backup arrived, we could easily end up trapped inside, dooming our entire project to a restart. And possibly dooming Cubism's dad to death. It made what was a routine size-up of a compound feel like it bore much more pressure than usual. If I was too aggressive in my assessment and bit off more than we could chew, we could all be killed. But if I was too conservative and said we didn't have a chance at this, we'd be set back as we tried to find an identical item elsewhere, which, for a legendary, could take ages.

I took a deep breath and tried to calm my heart, which had been accelerating. Dwelling on the consequences wasn't going to help me make a better decision. I'd made calls like this before, dozens of times. I usually got them right. I just needed to focus and think it through.

So, response time. The map didn't have a "find nearby structures" option, as convenient as that would have been at this particular moment, so I had to manually zoom out and pan around the area looking for the nearest base that looked like a likely candidate for the Unreals' reinforcements. I followed my typical search pattern: a quick pan in a circle around the area, then zoom out and pan around a larger, concentric circle until I found something. It was based on the idea that the locations of larger bases mattered more, so the further away the nearest base to the target was, the further zoomed out I could be and still identify it. It wasn't a perfect strategy, but it had a higher success rate than anything else I'd tried to use to approximate response times.

The nearest thing I found was a moderately sized shipyard, where the Unreals would store, repair, upgrade, and build their own custom ships. It had a large enough staff that it would likely be the location from which any rapid-response team was deployed. I did some rough calculations in my head, and figured we'd have about ten minutes before the response team arrived, which I rounded down to seven for safety. So I'd have to plan a mission to get us in and out, from first enemy contact to departure, in under seven minutes.

I panned back across the planet, taking another look at the bunker we needed to hit, and tried to gauge its size. Size, of course, wasn't a perfect indicator of how long it would take to search a building: a large facility might have an inventory that we could check and find our target instantly and a small building might be an absolute mess of junk that we'd have to practically swim through to find anything. Finally, it didn't tell me how many floors the building had, just the area of each floor. But, once again, it was a better way to determine how long we'd be in there than any other method I knew.

Using the "distance measurement" tool on my map told me that the building was about fifteen meters by twenty meters. There'd be five of us in there, and we could each search one floor. If there were more than five of levels to the building, we'd be screwed, but I didn't think it was likely. Seven minutes between arrival and extraction would give us opportunity to do a fast once-over of each level, in the worst-case scenario that there were five (if more than five, we'd do a hard abort and bail out of the mission entirely).

These uncertainties and risks weighed more heavily on me than usual due to the stakes, but I had to make a decision. I weighed the unknowns in my head: building depth, security, organization of the materials within. If any of these unknows was significantly more of a challenge than I planned for, the mission could easily fail.

I noticed an interesting feature of the bunker: it had roof access. There was a small protrusion out of the roof that I'd overlooked before, just enough space for a staircase down into the main area of the building. A plan started to take form in my head, a new way to assault the bunker.

I broke my silence with Cubism. "We can do it."

CHAPTER 22

It took under an hour for Cubism to gather the troops and for me to debrief them on our strategy. Soon after, Publius had us en route to the Nepthnar in his newly upgraded frigate. He'd spared no expense on the planetcrash capabilities of the vessel, but they'd go to waste here, as my attack strategy wouldn't permit it.

We planned to go into the building from the roof, and while Publius' shiny new planetcrash pods were capable of hitting targets that small, they'd hit with too much force, and we'd risk destroying the item we meant to extract. Instead, we'd be defying convention by landing slowly. We'd drop from the frigate in a space-combat suit with a parachute, then deploy the latter once we were under the radar shadow, manually finessing the landing onto the roof of the building. It was an unusual attack vector and should give us an immediate advantage in clearing the bunker of hostiles.

Cubism had tensed up again. I'd heard it in his voice when he'd started our planning meeting, and I now heard it in his silence.

The others didn't seem to notice. Jeremy and Marissa were chatting amiably, though Jessica, exuding her usual cold air, didn't join in. I wondered if she had something on the line the way Cubism did, or if she was just like that naturally. I didn't feel comfortable asking, so silence persisted among all of us but Jessica and Jeremy. I'd tried to join in their conversation, once, but I'd found myself too nervous. This was my first mission without a safety net: if I died here, it would all be over.

It seemed like an eternity before Publius had us in position to drop, our stealth systems engaged to prevent any early warning to the Unreals. As I stepped towards the drop door, my stress began to melt away. This was *PlanetCrash*, this was my expertise. It was foolish to fear having the course of my life depend on my skill, when I'd never worried during the times that I'd believed the course of my life was dependent on my performance in school. I was far more able to perform on this stage than that one.

"Everyone ready?" I asked the team. Nods and thumbs up were my response. "I'll drop first, followed by Jeremy, Marissa, Cubism and then Jessica, with Publius holding station. Count five seconds between each jump so that we have good separation. Good luck everyone."

I jumped.

Nepthnar was a small planet, its gravitational acceleration relatively weak compared to the many other worlds of *PlanetCrash*. Nevertheless, it almost immediately felt like my speed had gotten out of control. With no air to slow me down this high up, I fell faster and faster and my heart rate accelerated alongside my speed.

Traditional planetcrashes were second nature to me by now, but this novel way of deploying to a target from orbit was more far visceral than I was used to. Instead of being enclosed in a protective pod, I was exposed directly to the Nepthnarian atmosphere as I fell into it. The wind built in a crescendo as the air density increased throughout my fall, until it threatened to blow out my headphones.

A dot on my HUD represented the location of the bunker, or, more accurately, its nominal coordinates. The bunker itself was smaller than the target we could place, so we'd have to do some manual corrections once it came into view.

I tried to keep myself pointed in the general direction of the target, but was buffeted so aggressively by the turbulence that I was unable to control my own course. The atmosphere was now thick enough, however, that the drag began to slow me down. My altimeter's vertical speed indicator fell from over three hundred meters per second to two hundred, to one hundred, then finally levelled out at fifty: the lower-atmosphere's terminal velocity.

Velocity was less important than altitude, now. I had to wait to deploy my chute until we were under the radar horizon. Our best estimate was that their radar (if they had one at all) would be located at the shipyard nearby, the same place we expected their reinforcements to come from. Based on this, we'd calculated the radar horizon to be about one kilometer up. I was still three kilometers above that.

I deactivated my HUD marker: the bunker was visible to the naked eye now. Since hitting terminal velocity, my descent was much easier to control, so I was able to angle myself towards the bunker. I spun around momentarily to look above me and ensure the others had followed safely: sure enough, I could see Jeremy's outline a few hundred meters above me, with the others far enough away that they were barely distinguishable dots in the sky.

I flipped back around and corrected my course for the errors I'd caused with my rotation. I was now only two kilometers above the radar horizon: about forty seconds before parachute deployment at my current speed.

Those forty seconds felt like an eternity and I pulled my chute as soon as my altimeter read nine hundred ninety-nine meters. I felt another jerk of deceleration as the parachute caught me. I was directly overhead the bunker now and my speed was only seven meters per second. It'd be two and a half more minutes before I reached the target.

Oddly, this leisurely descent was even more stressful than the chaotic plummet which had preceded it. Even though I'd recolored the parachutes green to match the Nepthnarian skies before the assault, the hue wasn't perfect and if any of the guards happened to look directly up, it would be a simple matter for them to pick me off if they had a weapon that had any sort of accuracy at long range or if they'd put enough points into Precision. I knew logically that it was unlikely that they would, since orbital assaults were almost exclusively done with planetcrashes, and no guard could ever fail to notice a PC pod slamming into the ground at high speed, no matter where they were looking. The logic did nothing to calm my nerves, though.

I hit the roof of the bunker and rolled into the landing, equipping my grappling-hook pulse rifle and training it on the roof-access door to cover the others as they touched down, in case security had noticed the thud from my landing.

Jeremy arrived a few seconds later, instantly packing up his parachute back into its backpack. I itched to do the same, as having it still unravelled meant I was fighting the wind just to remain still. Usually, the first one down would cut their parachute, but that would cause the billowing fabric to blow off the roof and potentially into view of a guard. I didn't want to trigger the alarm any earlier than absolutely necessary. As soon as Jeremy finished packing up his parachute, he equipped his rifle and took up covering the door, allowing me to relax and collect my own chute. Marissa touched down shortly after.

About a minute later, the full team was on the roof, save Publius, who remained in the frigate above. Jeremy placed a breaching charge on the door and we clustered around the sides of the protrusion that connected the door to the stairway to stay out of the blast area. He detonated the charge and immediately I

139

took point descending the stairwell with my rifle raised. I reached the bottom of the stairs and kicked the door there open, allowing Jeremy to take up the point position.

"Contact!" he shouted, diving for cover as soon as he passed through the door. I was still in the doorframe when the guards opened fire and was forced to choose instantly whether to advance or retreat into cover as the first shots began filling the air with smoke, dust, and particles from the concrete walls that they blew holes in. I dove forward to take cover behind a pillar to the right-hand side of the door, then re-raised my rifle and shot blindly at the source of the enemy fire.

The room was dim, lit primarily by the flashes of energy emitting from our rifles. Rows and rows of shelves lined the interior, each doubtless home to dozens, if not hundreds, of items. I could make out several silhouettes at the opposite side of the room when I peeked out from behind my pillar, each sending shot after shot towards the door from which Jeremy and I had entered. Two of the others, probably Marissa and Jessica, had poked their guns around the doorway to return fire without exposing themselves.

No one seemed to be focused on me, so I dashed across to the next pillar to my right, to the next row of shelves. Looking to my left, Jeremy was behind a pillar similar to mine, but his well-placed shots had caused a few of the hostiles to target him. I was the only one of our team who could move around safely.

"Jeremy!" I shouted to get his attention over the gunfire. "Toss me a frag!"

Immediately, he ceased firing, pressing his back up against his pillar, then threw a grenade to me, sidearm. I caught it, then pushed further and further to the right-hand side, one pillar at a time.

As I reached the final pillar, the final row of items, I crouched low and dashed forward towards our enemies. I was far enough off to the side that none of the guards were within my sight and I hoped they'd lost track of me too. No one emerged around the corner to confront me as I advanced, so I guessed I was safe.

Momentarily, I wondered how the others were holding up. I hadn't explained my plan to them, and while I assumed they knew I wasn't just abandoning them, I was a little uncomfortable leaving the team. Hopefully, they would be well cared-for in Jeremy's hands.

I reached the end of the row. By now I should be parallel to the guards, but from my new angle there were several rows of shelves covering me from them. The shelves appeared broader here but side-on there were plenty of gaps to see through...Hopefully, the guards would be hesitant to shoot through the artifacts they were tasked to protect...

Pulling the pin from the grenade, I glanced around the corner at my targets. To my disappointment, they were spread fairly well apart, so I'd only be able to hit a couple of them with the 'nade. Still, it was the best ambush I had.

I chucked the grenade into the center of the guards, then requipped my rifle and unloaded at them. They panicked for a moment as I opened fire, taking a moment to realize where my shots were coming from before falling back out of the room and down their own staircase that connected the top floor to the rest of the bunker. Four bodies remained, though, taken down by my grenade or by the shots we'd fired into the fleeing guards. The killfeed showed two kills for me from my grenade, one for Marissa, and one for Jeremy.

"Room is clear, you can push up!" I called out and dashed over to the door through which the guards had fled. Jeremy jogged over to the door, standing across it from me and the rest of the team followed shortly after.

141

"Jessica, start searching this floor for the package. Everyone else, downstairs with me. We've been in here for a couple minutes already, we probably only have three more minutes until backup arrives. I want all the guards dead by then."

"I couldn't get a good count of them," Jeremy said. "Do you know how many are left?"

"I think six more," I replied. "Ten total, four down."

"Roger that."

"Let's move out."

I trotted downstairs, Jeremy directly behind me. We reached the floor directly below when I realized we didn't know which floor the guards had exited onto.

"Cube, watch the door. Everyone else, let's sweep through this floor real quick."

Each of us pushed through one of the rows of shelves, then returned via the adjacent row. None of the Unreal guards turned up, so we set Cubism onto searching the area while Marissa, Jeremy and I continued downstairs. It wouldn't do to split up further, though, as we were now back to being out-numbered two-to-one. But since the previous fight had proven that we had superior levels and equipment, I still wasn't worried.

The three of us swept through the two floors below, which also proved to be abandoned. We hit the ground floor and cleared that as well, all the way to a large metal door that was ajar, framed by green daylight. Evidently the guards had fled the building, hoping to retake it when reinforcements arrived. Little did they know that was exactly what we wanted...

Now that the bunker was cleared of hostiles, we started making the entryway as defensible as possible. Given that this was a bunker, there was only one entrance, which was already an excellent defensive position, but we did our best to enhance it. Jeremy and I toppled several of the shelves (leaving Marissa to

142

dig through the loot) and we jammed them into the entrance hallway. Not only would this make the entry door significantly harder to open, but even if it was opened it'd be difficult for anyone to crawl through the densely packed shelves to get into the bunker. If they tried to clear them out with explosives, that'd be a highly delicate task. Too high a yield would collapse the entry entirely, burying it in rubble, and too low wouldn't damage the shelves, which seemed to be made of solid steel.

With that completed to our satisfaction, we dashed back up both sets of staircases to return to the roof. As I'd expected, reinforcements were beginning to arrive now, I could see that they were setting up a forward operating base outside the bunker. They wanted to retake it with as little damage as possible done to the structure and its contents: that was our main advantage here. Otherwise they'd have just bombed the place. It took a moment before they noticed that we'd arrived at the top and they opened fire at us.

"HEY!" I shouted. "WE WANT TO NEGOTIATE!"

The shooting stopped. The Unreals seemed confused: they weren't prepared for this. It took a few minutes before someone shouted back.

"There are five of you and dozens of us already here, with more on the way. Why should we negotiate?"

"We've got the whole place rigged to blow," I responded. "If you want to see anything you've got in storage here ever again, you'll want to talk to us!"

This, as it happened, was a pure bluff. I'd briefly considered actually using such a tactic as a way to get us out, but there had been two critical problems: first, the amount of explosives necessary to blow the entire place had been prohibitively expensive. We simply couldn't afford it. Second, it was a terrible risk. If we had to detonate the explosives, all of our characters would be

143

instantly killed and the project would collapse. Fortunately, the Unreals didn't know who we were, what our resources were, or the nature of our project. For all they knew, we were an expendable squad of newbies from a powerful faction on exactly such a suicide mission.

"Let's say I believe you," the Unreal called. "What do you want?"

"We want you to cede some territory to Resistance faction! One star system specifically: Barron Alpha!"

Earlier, we'd chewed over the right demand for this bluff. It had to be something reasonable enough that they wouldn't immediately decide to sacrifice their supply bunker, but extreme enough that they wouldn't be too quick to accept. Bringing up the Resistance faction was a clever idea that Jessica had added when we'd been discussing this. Resistance were dedicated to ensuring that no other factions became strong enough to impose their will onto the majority of the server, essentially trying to prevent any Ultimate Empires from arising. They inevitably failed, but they certainly slowed down the progression of the large factions to UEs.

"I don't have the authority to do that. I'll pass it up the chain, but is there anything else we could do to work this out?"

"Nothing comes to mind," I replied. "Feel free to make offers and let me know when your superiors get back to you."

In the distance, I could see another group of troops approaching in armored personnel carriers. We'd graduated from the Unreals' rapid response team and soon there would be over a hundred hostiles surrounding the bunker. It was more than enough to take us out, but not enough to do so without destroying much of what was stored here: even if they didn't believe we had the place rigged to blow, the collateral damage would still be immense. Still, knowing how easily they could kill us, I shivered. My plan needed to work.

Jeremy and I exited the rooftop and went back down into the bunker. We'd seen what we needed to see and hopefully stalled the Unreals long enough for us to track down the target. I'd also taken care to tell them that we'd be willing to accept other diplomatic solutions than our single demand. Doubtless, their field commander would be trying to think something up that would sound good to the higher-ups in the faction in an after-action report. We'd intentionally made ourselves hard to contact after that, though, so that they wouldn't realize we didn't want to accept any offer that they made. We just wanted to stall.

Cubism jogged over to us. "Top floor is clear. Negative on the target."

I nodded. "Go down two; Jessica is working the one below us."

It took over an hour of searching before Marissa secured the package. For that entire time, I'd been alternating between checking in with the team on their search progress, making a show of negotiation with the Unreals outside, and just pacing anxiously. Finally, though, we were ready to move, ready to see whether my screwball plan would be a success. I placed a call up to Publius, requesting extraction.

Now that we had the target in hand (a legendary engine piece, used to build especially speedy corvettes), we all moved up towards the roof. We didn't leave the stairwell, though, as we weren't ready for that yet. Jeremy had procured a carbon fiber cable, similar to the material that my grappling rifle had attached to its hook, on one of his personal missions and he used it to link all of us together as we waited for extraction. It was a bit of a risky play, as being tied to the others on a short length of cable would reduce my mobility, but it would ensure that none of us was left behind in the chaos that was about to occur.

Publius gave the signal that he was thirty seconds out and we moved from the stairwell onto the roof, being careful to stay low, hopefully low enough that we wouldn't be visible from the ground.

I handed Marissa my rifle. She was the best shot of all of us—it was her job to be—so if anyone could make this plan work, it would be her. She took it without a word, her usual friendliness likely silenced by the same nerves that quieted the rest of us.

The sound of Publius flying in at supersonic speeds started quietly in the distance, but quickly grew to a deafening roar. He didn't have his horizontal thrusters active, just the verticals, so the air resistance bled through his momentum quickly, until he was moving at a much more reasonable speed as he flew overhead.

He was flying low, only about a hundred feet over our heads, but he was still only overhead for less than a second. In that time, though, Marissa squeezed off a shot from my grappling rifle, attaching us to the bottom of the corvette. The two carbon fiber cables were immensely strong, and yanked the five of us off of the bunker roof without ever straining. As soon as we were attached, Publius gunned the forward thrusters and accelerated back up to blistering speeds, dragging the rest of us beneath him, away from the Unreals. They fired at us as we disappeared, of course, but we were small, fast moving, and far away: the hat trick for being hard to hit.

Once we'd cleared the range of their weapons, Publius slowed down again and lowered us to the ground. We scrambled to get properly onboard the ship, knowing that Unreal interception aircraft were likely already inbound.

We hadn't given them enough time to scramble their interceptors, though and we had cleared the atmosphere and jumped to lightspeed before any other ships arrived.

Once in lightspeed, tension melted away from my body, and the stressed atmosphere of the team was instantly replaced with one of relief. It was the typical post-mission euphoria, our limbs shaking with adrenaline as we congratulated each other on a successful raid.

Jessica's coldness bled away for the first time that I could remember, her avatar smiling at me. "That was an awesome plan," she said. "I still can't believe we pulled that off."

"Hell, yeah we did!" Jeremy shouted. "We're the best!" I hadn't ordered my avatar to mimic the expression, but back in the library I felt myself smiling like an idiot.

As agreed, Publius flew the ship back to a non-combat zone, where we wouldn't need to fear losing our stash of items to player attacks. This wasn't feasible as a strategy for large factions, who would then need to worry about transporting equipment to and from their home territory (hence why the Unreals had bunkers on a planet under their control, rather than the foolproof protection we were afforded). It was a major mechanic that allowed small, indie factions to continue to exist when so much of the galaxy was dominated by Empires, something which would inevitably develop as the server reached its endgame.

Once completely secure and still glowing with a sense of achievement, we each disconnected from the game and I returned to the library, and the real world.

CHAPTER 23

I fell into a routine over the next few days and my life stabilized around it. There were two central points to it: first, climbing the duel ladder with Jeremy, and second, avoiding Ezra. Jeremy and I had a great deal of success and after a few weeks, just before the tournament ended, we broke the top ten. Our ability to treat *PlanetCrash* as a full-time job gave us a massive advantage over the competition. Other competitors had just as much natural skill, but we were able to get ahead of them with the sheer number of hours we put in. Since the league benefitted the teams that competed the most, there was a direct advantage to this, alongside the improvement in our teamwork that came with it. We cashed out on a motherlode of EC and exp, enough to level each of us several times, and to fund another equipment upgrade spending spree, which I kept forgetting to actually go on. By the time the competition was over, between it and the occasional raid with the team, I'd hit level 30. I was splitting points pretty evenly between Agi, Str, and Pre now. Agi was still comfortably ahead of the others from my early level binge, but that was how I wanted it. Speed was key in a firefight. It was crazy how fast we were levelling compared to the average player. The server had only opened a few weeks ago and most players were still sub-10.

The other half of my life though…that I was less happy about. I felt it necessary to avoid Ezra whenever I wasn't at the library and I could hardly endure it. The only other person my age living at the SHU and I couldn't interact with him for fear of being told off again.

This ate at me for the weeks following our confrontation, growing worse and worse until it was almost all I could think about when outside *PlanetCrash*. Eventually, though, I broke, and realized I needed to talk to Ezra again, to explain myself. The source of his judgement was that he felt I wasn't doing anything to improve my life, right? Well I was. I was risking everything on a plan to do just that: that's why I was here! Ezra had wanted me to just get back to where I'd started, but my plan was to launch myself into a place of wealth far beyond what I had dreamed possible before it was staring me in the face. I remembered, of course, that Cubism had given us strict orders *not* to tell anyone outside of the team what was happening, due to the information security risk. And I understood his concerns there. But if he could kick Val from our team, creating not only a breach of that security, but one that had a grudge against us, then I could tell one person in order to win him over into supporting me.

I also toyed with the idea of mentioning Cubism's father to Ezra, when we had our talk. After all, Ezra seemed to be a moral kind of guy and saving someone's life would probably impress him more than talking about money. But maybe not. It would just sound fake, like a made up reason to win Ezra over. It just wouldn't work.

The day that Jeremy and I received our rewards from our placement in the league we'd joined, I was filled with a sense of empowerment and as I left the library for the evening, I resolved to speak with Ezra that very night. He wouldn't be difficult to find. I'd memorized his schedule as part of my effort to avoid him and it was easy enough to turn that same knowledge around and find him.

Dinner would be the easiest opportunity. Ezra regularly ate around the same time I got home from the library (at 9:30), and I'd forced myself to hold back my hunger for a half an hour extra each night to ensure that he'd left the dining hall.

Tonight, however, I strode into dinner as soon as I got back to the SHU. Sure enough, Ezra was there, eating alone as usual. I'd never thought of it this way before, but in confronting me, in standing up for his beliefs that I was wrong, he'd thrown away his only chance at a friend in the SHU. Just the same as my loss. He was missing key information, of course, that I wasn't, so in my mind he was justified in denouncing me like he had, even though he was dead wrong.

I got my own food before approaching him. The conversation would go better if I didn't have an empty stomach, right? But if I was being totally honest with myself, I had to admit that the real reason for going over to the counter and then to my own table was to give myself time to subdue the nerves that had grown as my confidence from earlier had faded.

Despite my later start, I still managed to finish my food before Ezra did his. I'd watched him from across the room during my meal. He ate very methodically, deliberately, even, as though he was carefully considering each bite. I, on the other hand, essentially shoveled food into my mouth as fast as I could, a habit built by years of knowing that *PlanetCrash* waited as soon as I'd finished my dinner. It wasn't necessary anymore, of course, but habits were hard to break.

I collected my plate and silverware to bus my table just after Ezra did, walking behind him to the dishwashing area. As we dropped off our dishes with the resident who was washing them today, Ezra noticed me at last.

"Can we talk?" I asked before he had a chance to react to seeing me again.

150

He hesitated, eyeing me as he considered his response. I didn't know what was going through his head, but I could imagine him weighing the possibility of having a friend here against his worry that he'd just end up indirectly validating me in my "video-game addiction," as he saw it. After a few seconds he caved…at least for the moment.

"Sure." His reply was obviously wary, but did I detect hints of hopefulness underneath? Or was that just wishful thinking?

We left the mess hall together so we could talk somewhere more private and ended up walking down to Moakley Park, which was a few blocks away from the SHU.

"I want to start by saying that, fundamentally, I agree with you," I began. "You're right that I should be trying to get back on my feet and improve my life. Where we differ…I know things about myself that you don't."

From there, I told Ezra everything. My late-night *Planet-Crash* sessions, how they'd interfered with school occasionally, my unhappy relationship with my parents, then meeting Cubism and finding a path that could bring me to financial independence through *PlanetCrash*. It had been a godsend to me, I emphasized. I told him our plan, the basics of how the exploit worked, though I left out any details that would allow him to go to the developers or use it himself. It never hurt to be careful. I even talked him through my journey within Cubism's team, how I'd killed Val and she'd been thrown out, and how I feared for my own ability to stay on the team if I hadn't run away from home. He listened through all of my explanation in silence, leaving me mystified at what he was thinking throughout. When I finished, though, he spoke up.

"So you're robbing thousands of people out of their life savings. Am I supposed to feel better about this?"

"No!" Hadn't I already explained this? I must have forgotten to mention it. "Every player's money is insured by the

151

FDIC, which itself is funded by the banks. We're just taking a few dollars back from the megabanks that have screwed us for years."

He snorted with derision. "That's a nice talking point you've got, but you're full of crap. The FDIC doesn't even insure against robbery, only against banks collapsing."

Ezra's words hit me like a bullet. "What?"

"That's just not how the FDIC works, Emily."

"Are you sure?"

"You've got a phone. Look it up. Honestly, I can't believe you haven't before now."

Sure enough, a quick internet search verified his claim. I slumped to the ground in shock. How had I not thought to check this before now?

"You didn't know, did you…" Ezra's voice changed, pity creeping in, and he chucked sadly. "You poor idiot. Go back to your old life. It's not too late."

"Not yet," I whispered. "I need to make sure the others know, too."

He nodded. "Shut this whole thing down, then go home."

CHAPTER 24

I called Cubism as soon as I'd regained my composure.

"Cube, you gotta shut the project down." I didn't waste any time getting to the point.

"What, *why*?" He was incredulous, of course, that I was coming at him for once, rather than the other way around.

"The money…it's not insured."

"Didn't we talk about this on the first day? The FDIC will reimburse the people for their money."

"It *won't*! The FDIC only protects against bank insolvency, not robbery!"

Silence hung between us for almost a minute. I could hear Cube's breathing as it shortened and quickened. Probably he was frantically searching online, trying to find out whether Ezra was right or for some loophole that would allow…

"You think I didn't already know that?" Cubism asked, his voice tight. "I don't care, Julia. Will people lose money? Sure. Tough, it happens. My father's life is on the line and I'm not just going to stand by as he grows closer to death every day. I'm going to do something, goddamn it, and I don't care what the cost is! Now if you want to shut up and get rich, the offer is still open. But if you want to give that up and be just another obstacle in my path, then I'll find a replacement for you as quickly as I did for Val."

I was stunned. While I hadn't been able to imagine what Cubism's reaction would be, I had not expected that he'd so blatantly blow this off. I certainly wasn't prepared to hear that he'd always known, that he'd been hiding information from us.

The one-two punch was too much to handle and I disconnected from my call with Cubism without another word. My world had been upended again, just as it had started to stabilize. Could I just ignore this? Cubism was right: his father's life was on the line. Or was it? Could I trust that story, knowing he'd lied before? Besides which, what of the people who we would be robbing? It was one thing when it'd been the banks, who made money hand over fist anyway. These were just ordinary people now. How many of them needed that money for their own medical bills? Or for next month's rent payment so they wouldn't end up in a SHU like me? Or worse, if they didn't live in a place where everyone was guaranteed housing by the government.

It was a terrible choice to be asked to make. The life of one man against the security of many. Why was I the one burdened to decide? Was it a karmic retribution for believing myself ready to forge my own path, throwing off the guidance of my parents?

I tried to shake these thoughts of the nature of choice from my head as the over-emotional melodrama that my logic told me they were, but they were stuck fast. Lying awake for hours, I struggled to choose. My decision, when it arrived, was motivated not by finding the morally correct answer, but rather by simple selfishness: I knew that if I returned to my work with Cubism and the scam was successful, there was a risk Ezra would learn about it and that would lead the police to me. Even if we got the money, I would go to prison.

Once the decision was made (albeit based on my own self-interest), I was filled with a sense of calm determination and knowledge that it was the right thing to do. And at the same time, a weight lifted from my shoulders that I hadn't even realized was there. I must have known, somewhere deep down, that this was too good to be true, but had refused to see it until now.

Cubism would be stopped; he had to be. And I would be the one to do it. With that thought, sleep came at last.

My new mission began the next morning and it was sure to be much easier than the last. All I had to do to put an end to this was submit a bug report to *PlanetCrash* Studios. They had a website for this and while they must get dozens, if not hundreds of reports every week, I was sure mine would stand out. I could provide a detailed description of how to reproduce the issue (unlike many bugs which players only saw by their result rather than their trigger: making diagnosis much more difficult for the developers) and it was a security-related issue. I was confident it would be patched out of the game within days, if not hours. Cubism wouldn't have enough time to finish collecting the necessary items and the people of the server would be safe from him.

As per my previous routine, I arrived at the library promptly as it opened and dashed as fast as the librarians would allow into the teens-only section. After logging in, I navigated to the *PlanetCrash* website to find the bug report page. It was there, I knew from others, but I'd never actually used it myself. *Planet-Crash* was a very stable game, and I'd never encountered anything that needed reporting before now.

When I found the page, it was a simple form that I had to fill out.

```
Email address:

Description    of    issue/instructions    for
reproduction:
```

155

```
Record and attach video of issue: Upload

Submit Form
```

I didn't have any video, of course, but I filled out the other two sections quickly enough, giving all of the details for the exploit that I knew, including the full list of items you'd need in your inventory. I clicked "Submit Form," confident that it would be the end of this entire affair.

Instead, I got an error message:

```
Could not submit form! The following required
sections are missing and/or blank: Video of
Issue

Please upload a video of the bug in action.
Without that, it's incredibly difficult to
determine what the issue is.

Thanks!

PlanetCrash Studios
```

Well, it seemed we weren't out of the woods yet.

I clicked over to the generic contact page. There was a customer support phone number there, though no email address. I ignored the disclaimer that it was not to be used for technical support issues—figuring that this was important enough that they wouldn't mind a minor misuse—and dialed the number.

The call connected me with a robotic answering service, of course, and I immediately started sifting through its menus, searching for a way to speak with a person. About an hour later, I gave up hope on that path, thoroughly convinced that Planet-Crash Studios' customer support was entirely automated, like so many were now.

Perhaps a forum post? I toyed with the idea but rejected it. There were too many of those, and anyone with enough computer savviness to believe my story would have the key to the scam themselves. It wasn't worth the risk. The idea transitioned into another in my mind: one that wouldn't require me to give away details about the vulnerability.

I was perversely glad all this hadn't worked, in a way, despite the wasted time, as I dreaded going back to my family. There was only one solution left for this problem: I was going to have to put together my own team and activate the exploit before Cubism could.

CHAPTER 25

Cubism had a head start, of course, but I had two significant advantages. First, I didn't need to worry about "share dilution" and could bring on as many people as I wanted: if Cubism tried the same, he'd end up without enough money to pay for his dad's treatment (or his own gain, if that was a story). So there was a hard cap on how large his team could be. Once I got a numbers advantage, I'd have a core group dedicated to hunting down the necessary artifacts and the rest of my followers could simply focus on making it impossible for Cubism's team to make any progress: assaulting and harassing them whenever possible.

My second advantage was that I could probably just steal Cubism's team out from under him. It seemed unlikely that any of them would place their own financial gain over the security of tens of thousands of *PlanetCrash* players, so I was confident they'd all defect with me. Since most of the items were stored on Publius' ship, Cubism would be set back to square one.

The first call I placed was to Jeremy, of course. He'd be the easiest to get, since I was much closer to him than the others. Once he was on my side, the two of us together would more convincing than I was alone.

Jeremy picked up almost instantly. "Hey Julia! You ready to get some more grinding in?"

I ignored the questions, laser-focused on my new mission. "Not right now. We need to talk about something."

The upbeat tone he usually held drained from his voice as he heard the worry and stress in mine. "Okay. What's up?"

"Cubism's been lying to us this whole time." I explained my conversations with Ezra and Cubism. Jeremy was silent while I talked, obviously troubled by the information.

When I told him about my failed attempt to report the bug, Jeremy took a minute to curse to himself before addressing me. "So what do we do?" He asked. "We can't stop him if the devs won't accept your report. But it doesn't feel right to continue...honestly it never felt totally right. I just didn't think about it much."

I nodded. "We were just playing a game. But now it's more than that."

"What now?"

"I think we can stop him," I replied. "Just not in real life."

"What do you mean?"

"Harass him in-game. His team, and anyone who joins them. We'll get as many of the items as we can, then trigger the glitch ourselves, without taking anyone's money, and submit the bug report once we have the video evidence."

"Yeah...yeah, that could work. We're gonna need a bigger team, though."

"I know. I was hoping we could sway some of the others to our side. I was going to call Marissa next, can you talk to Publius?"

"Sure. What about Jessica?"

"Jessica is his spymaster. I wouldn't trust her on our side either way."

"Makes sense."

159

"I will get in touch with Val, though. Hopefully her grudge is against Cubism, and not me."

That made Jeremy laugh, some of his tension breaking. "Killing her was still really dumb of you."

I ignored him, not wanting to think about it. "And then I'm going to put out a call for general recruitment."

"You're *what*?"

"We need to have people ready around the clock in case Cubism makes a move. Besides which, no one on this server wants their money stolen. It shouldn't be that hard to outnumber them massively, make it impossible for Cubism to go into a PvP zone without getting killed."

Jeremy seemed hesitant. I didn't know why. "I...guess that makes sense? I don't know, it just feels weird to blow this wide open after keeping it secret for so long."

"I get what you mean," I replied. "But there's no reason to keep this under wraps anymore. The more people who know, the better, I think. People have a right to know if their money is on the line."

"I worry that some people will move their money into another account. Then Cubism will only be stealing from the people who are entirely dependent on a single account, and will wipe them out entirely. Or that some third party will get involved and rush to use the exploit themselves, someone we don't know to watch."

He had a good point, much the same as I was worried about. "I'll have to think about it, but I'm confident I can come up with some way of getting people on our side without giving too much away. In the meantime, we should get talking to the others."

"Right-o." We broke off the call to talk to our various targets.

160

My conversation with Marissa was far quicker than the one with Jeremy. She was immediately horrified when I broke the news to her and agreed to defect, with two provisions: first, that she would confirm that Cubism had lied with her own research into the FDIC, and second, that I not have Cubism's stringent hours requirements.

"I'll need to get a job, now," she explained. "Since I can't rely on your operation to pay the bills down the road."

This was another consideration: without the financial incentive that Cubism could promise (and threaten to take away), it would be much harder—if not impossible—to get as much of a time commitment out of my followers. Another reason why we needed more people.

After my talk with Marissa, I checked in again with Jeremy, who reported that Publius wouldn't be joining us. It was our first failure and a big one: with several of the rare items required for the exploit stored on Publius' ship, Cubism was safe from experiencing any material losses to his progress: only personnel ones.

Still, I hoped my revolt would slow Cubism down. Unfortunately, our failure to encourage Publius to defect would mean that as of now, Cubism would know that the rest of us were turning away and he would likely begin trying to find replacements immediately.

Val wasn't online, likely because of school, so I sent her a message asking her to call me. I wasn't sure if she'd respond. Did she blame me for her kick from the team, or Cubism? I had no way of knowing: I hadn't spoken to her since I'd killed her. It felt like forever since I had, even though it had been less than a month. So much had changed since then.

That done, I called a meeting for all the defectors from Cubism and set up a new Discord server for us before Cubism could ban us from the old.

As Jeremy and Marissa connected, I realized with a sense of dread that I'd made myself the de facto leader of this group and would have to act accordingly.

"Uh…Hello guys," I began. "I think the first, um, thing we need to talk about is how big our resistance against Cubism should be: whether we should bring in new people, and, uh, how many."

"Woah, hold up a second," Jeremy cut in. "Before we start with all that serious stuff, we need a name. What are we gonna call ourselves?"

I should have been annoyed by the distraction from meaningful topics, but in truth I was relieved. Jeremy took attention away from my fumbling attempt to run the meeting, and, when I thought about it, he was right: if we were going to recruit, we'd need a strong name. Even if we weren't going to, it'd help to have some way to talk about ourselves. This had been one oversight on Cubism's part: not giving us a strong enough name to identify with. The Ocean Project, he'd initially called it, but he never used that name since. We'd just been his followers.

The other two debated the merits of various names for far longer than was practical, but I didn't step in to offer my opinions or try to stop them. I was scared to step back into the spotlight of this meeting, and the longer this debate went on, the better.

It didn't last as long as I'd hoped, though, as they also knew that this issue of a name was only tangentially important. They settled on Artemis, named for the Greek god of hunters, since we planned to hunt the items for the glitch and Cubism. Also, because we liked the way it sounded.

That distraction over, it was much easier to segue back into the real matter at hand: the pros and cons of expanding Artemis, as our efforts would now be called.

162

Jeremy lead off the debate, reiterating his points from before: the danger of uncontrolled information and the possibility that we'd inadvertently create more risk for account holders. His proposal was to restrict the theft only to those who could least afford it.

Marissa argued the opposite. She knew, from her own life, that she wouldn't be able to put in the time that Cubism's followers would and neither would Val (should she join us). Without being able to match Cubism's team for time, the only way to compensate would be superior numbers.

I moderated this debate for a while, before realizing it was ultimately pointless. I'd already made up my mind and Marissa clearly supported me. Jeremy was outvoted. Besides, if I had to be the "leader" of Artemis, then I should at least get to make decisions, shouldn't I?

We broke the meeting when Jeremy relented, realizing that it was two against one and he was unlikely to convince either of us.

CHAPTER 26

To start our open recruitment, I realized I'd have to make a post in *PlanetCrash*'s Looking For Group forums. It would give away any element of surprise we currently had over Cubism, but the numbers advantage would likely prove far more valuable.

I started a new topic in the LFG forum and began typing.

```
Join Artemis—Protectors of the NA-22 Server!

Artemis is a new faction dedicated to a new
type of defense of the server. We've
discovered a glitch that, if exploited in-
game, could allow another player to take money
from your bank account without your
permission. For information security, I will
not give specifics in this post. Our goals are
twofold: to ensure that no one is able to
abuse this glitch and to activate the glitch
ourselves, without taking any money, so that
we can have the video evidence required to
submit a bug report to PlanetCrash studios.

Unfortunately, there is another group,
formerly allied with Artemis' founders, which
is determined to exploit this bug to rob you.

We must stop them by hunting them down and
anyone else who attempts to steal from the NA-
22 community.

Will you join us?
```

I submitted the post without rereading or editing it. There was nothing I hated more than reading my own writing, it always felt awkward and dumb.

Thankfully, the post seemed to work: within minutes I was receiving messages from players who were interested in joining my new faction. I was surprised to find that many of them didn't believe that the glitch existed and treated Artemis like a role-playing group, like we were only *pretending* that there was a security issue. It made sense: I don't think I would have believed my post either. Besides which, I was happy to take this. If people thought we were just RPing, it would mitigate some of the risk of defectors who might try to exploit the glitch in a breakaway party.

I responded to each of the messages personally, inviting each of the players to our new Discord server, welcoming them to Artemis, and asking about their skills. Two hours after my post went up, ten new members had joined Artemis, with a diverse set of skills. The Discord server's text chat was filled with fast-moving conversation of introductions and light bragging. It was the vibrant atmosphere that most factions in *PlanetCrash* offered and which I'd almost forgotten in the stressed and desperate environment of Cubism's team, where I'd only really been able to talk to Jeremy comfortably.

My next priority, though, was to determine who our spymaster would be. We'd need to be able to contend with Jessica, who, while not an expert, was certainly more than competent in the field of information gathering and had proven especially resourceful in the most critical area of her job: tracking down the necessary items.

I flipped through my message threads with the people I'd recruited so far, eventually favoring a player whose in-game name was Chris Stewart. He'd worked in intelligence in several major factions on previous servers, including some UEs. In fact,

165

from what he'd said, I'd guessed he was the one who'd been responsible for the battle in which I'd died on the previous server: he'd determined that the United Front had been planning a surprise attack on the Cerulean's homeworld and capital, which caused the Ceruleans to pull back all their ships for a defense. Both empires had fallen after that battle, as I'd predicted at the time, which left thousands of players like Chris looking for new factions on new servers.

Even if he wasn't the best pick to run our spy network, he certainly knew how to work inside it, and I could replace him later if need be. I sent him a direct message to ask if he'd be interested in the position and when he'd confirmed I brought him up to speed on a couple more details on the glitch. Not enough for him to activate it himself (probably), but I did give him the full list of items needed, tasking him both to look out for them and also to keep up-to-date on what Cubism was planning.

"That's a bit big of a job for just one person," he commented.

He had a point. "You can take any two others as your subordinates. I'll give you more when Artemis grows."

Chris accepted that and immediately got to work trying to determine which of our members would be his spies.

Soon after we'd finished that conversation, Val responded to my ping from earlier, initiating a call with me.

"Hi Val," I said, feeling anxious as I connected.

"Hi Julia!" she replied, bubbling with the same energy she always seemed to have (except for the time I'd killed her).

"How've you been?" I asked. In my conversations with Publius and Cubism, I'd skipped over small talk to get directly to the matter at hand. With Val, though, I wanted to take some time to get a sense of her. The other two I'd interacted with frequently before my discovery, but Val I hadn't talked to in weeks. From her voice, she didn't seem like she was upset with

166

me, but I'd made a plan and although conversations weren't like combat: if I made a plan, I pretty much had to stick to it or fall apart.

"Oh, I'm doing great!" Val responded, her distinctive Mexican accent colouring each word. "I was really sad when Cubism kicked me out, of course, and mad at you for killing me, but really everything's been going a lot smoother since I quit *PlanetCrash*! My grades instantly improved: I haven't gotten an A-minus in weeks! So I thought to myself, what's to be mad about? Cubism and Julia helped me with my studies!"

"That's great, Val; I'm glad things are going well." A confusing mix of emotions washed over me. I was relieved that Val didn't have a grudge against me, of course, and I was happy to hear that her life was going well outside of *PlanetCrash*. I'd liked Val, for the short time I'd known her. She'd infected me with her enthusiasm for, well, just about everything. She managed to sound relentlessly positive even when complaining or venting about her problems. I'd hated knowing that I'd destroyed that positivity when I'd killed her and driven her to tears, but it was a great relief to find out that she had bounced back from that so quickly.

All that said, she seemed all too happy to be *gone* from *PlanetCrash*. Would she come back if I asked her? Did I even want her to? Could I justify asking her to possibly sacrifice her performance in school to help Artemis?

I decided to tell her what was going on. She was just a kid, sure, but she had the right to make her own decision about whether to be involved. Val didn't need me to protect her, as much as I might have wanted to.

Bringing her up to speed took longer than with any of those I'd previously spoken to. Not seeing where this story ended, she'd insisted on a recap of everything that had happened since she'd left: recruiting Marissa; how I'd almost died trying to

167

board the pirates' ship; our bunker raid...so much had happened.

It was relieving, in a way, to talk through everything. Jeremy and I had often left this "business" unsaid when we'd trained together, especially when we had fought in the league. Our conversations had focused almost exclusively on tactics and improving our place on the leaderboard. I'd never spoken aloud before about what had happened and it had been weighing on me. Holding the stress, victories, and defeats all inside of me with no release was something I'd never done before. On previous servers, I'd been part of large enough alliances that someone I liked would want to be brought up to date on whatever my latest operation had been and would share their stories as well. I hadn't gotten that on here though. The pursuit of wealth had necessitated that we not share information.

It also helped, of course, that Val was a great audience. She understood the firefights of *PlanetCrash* in the same way I did and was suitably impressed at how I'd tackled each problem I'd faced. And, of course, when I told her the truth, that Cubism was stealing from all of us, and not just a few megabanks, she was furious in a way that I barely believed was possible for her.

Val let out a frantic barrage of Spanish, an unfamiliar edge in her voice. I didn't know what she was saying: I'd taken Latin in school, but I didn't need it to guess that if I recorded her words and looked them up, I'd have a pretty comprehensive vocabulary of Spanish curses.

It took a minute before she'd calmed down enough to switch back to English.

"I'm sorry," she said. "I just can't believe Cubism would do this..."

"I know," I replied. "When I confronted him about it, he didn't deny it, he just mentioned..." I hesitated, momentarily unsure of whether to tell Val about Cubism's father and possibly

168

win her sympathy "…mentioned that he needed the money for family reasons." Well, it wasn't a lie.

"Still! He's a liar and a thief." She paused. "I guess he hasn't given up, though, even though you called him out?"

"Unfortunately not," I replied. "I think he's more determined than ever…That's why Jeremy and I have started a faction to stop him."

"You're planning to kill Cubism?" Val asked.

"Him, and anyone who works for him, and anyone who holds more than one of the items needed for the exploit. From now until the day that *PlanetCrash* Studios find and fix this."

"Wow," Val said. "Can I join?"

"Of course!" Thank God, I hadn't even had to ask her. She'd just offered, even though she knew she was likely to slip back in her grades (to A-minus range, I supposed—the horror!), she stood up to help us. Val was incredible.

I sent her the link to the Artemis Discord server. "Welcome back to *PlanetCrash.*"

CHAPTER 27

I returned to the SHU early that evening, even though I knew I should be busier than ever with all of the work there still was ahead of me. So much of the day had been spent organizing Artemis: talking to people, convincing them to join or to lead, and it had been an exhausting success. There was more to be done, but I needed a break and hoped to see Ezra.

He would probably be at the SHU when I got home, as he'd had the day off from work. I hoped he'd be willing to hang out with me: I didn't know where our relationship stood at this point, given everything that had happened.

As it happened, he was walking out just as I arrived.

"Oh hey, Emily!" Ezra seemed genuinely happy to see me, in a way that I'd never heard before. My parents and friends from school always seemed to be very neutral about my presence, at best. It was also a relief: the fear that he'd be angry or judgemental faded away from me.

"Hey, Ezra," I smiled. "Where are you headed? Work?" I knew it wasn't true, but I didn't want Ezra to know how much effort I'd gone to in learning his schedule to avoid him. It seemed so childish now, so embarrassing. I wished I'd confided in him earlier, which would have saved so much time...

"Actually, I'm just heading out for a walk. Care to join me?"

170

I was surprised to find that my exhaustion had melted away and that I did feel up to a stroll. "Absolutely," I replied.

As we walked aimlessly through South Boston, I brought him up to speed on the progress I'd made in *PlanetCrash* that day. He didn't say much, but from his occasional remark I thought I could detect a conflict within him: one part of him realizing that fighting Cubism was the right thing to do, the other just wanting me to drop it and look out for myself. It was a conflict I'd struggled with, but I didn't know how to talk about it directly with him, so I changed the subject just as we were arriving at the Summer Street Bridge.

"I know this is kind of taboo," I began, "but I am wondering how you ended up in the SHU with me."

He stopped. We were halfway across the bridge, which spanned a small piece of the bay that cut into the city, like the mouth of a river that wasn't there.

"I like to sit here," Ezra said, hopping onto the guardrail. "And think. It relaxes me."

I climbed up beside him, hanging my legs over the dark water below, waiting.

"I ran away from home," he replied after a minute or two of silence. "My father drank a lot, used to beat the crap out of me each night. Repressed anger about mom leaving or some BS. It doesn't matter. I couldn't stay there. So I just…didn't come home from school one day. I didn't know this place existed when I left, so I spent a week and a half on the street, begging, before someone told me. Everything's stabilized since then…I don't even think about him anymore, most days."

My heart broke as I listened to him. Ezra had kept his voice perfectly neutral as he'd talked, and I guessed he was trying to hide the pain that I'd brought up. I couldn't see his expression in the dark, his face cast in the shadow of his long, black hair, but I could imagine the hurt in his eyes. A wave of guilt washed

171

over me. Ezra shouldn't have had to relive those experiences just because I was curious. Now I really understood why asking about people's past was taboo in the SHU. Some people offered their history, to let it out, and that was fine, but no one asked. No one wanted to bring up memories like this.

I wanted desperately to comfort Ezra, to find some way to alleviate his pain, but I couldn't. I didn't know if any words could help him, and which ones would if they could. "How long has it been? Since you left?"

He considered for a moment. "A little under three years."

I let that sink in. He'd been living in the SHU that long? It was almost unbelievable. Most people in the SHU that I'd talked to were constantly looking to get out. The adults would start searching for a different place to live whenever they landed jobs. No one had resided here continuously for three years, not that I'd spoken with. That meant that, paradoxically, Ezra was both the youngest and the oldest resident of the SHU.

I let him steer the conversation away after that, to lighter matters. But the pain didn't leave his eyes all the way back.

CHAPTER 28

Over the next few days, as Artemis grew, I settled into a new routine. First thing in the morning I'd head over to the library, log in to *PlanetCrash* and get an intelligence update from Chris. So far those had been boring: Cubism wasn't very active. We'd lost track of Jessica, so we didn't know what leads they might have had, but they hadn't deployed anywhere since the schism. I hoped that, in this case, no news was good news. Perhaps they'd hit a roadblock without us even needing to intervene.

The next thing on my schedule was overseeing Artemis' growth. We were getting new members every day, as word spread and people got their friends on board. I tried to send each new member a greeting, acutely aware of how unwelcome Cubism had made me feel. There was no reason to be rude, I felt, no matter how stressed I got. So I made the effort to be friendly and available to our new members. Beyond that, I appointed Jeremy as the head of our fleets, which currently consisted of only five capital ships. It was still far more than Cubism could muster, though, so I felt it would be enough. Jeremy had about thirty crewmen, half of Artemis' members, serving under him. Most of the remainder were marines under Marissa and her second-in-command, Val. Marissa had done good work so far, claiming a small moon to serve as our home base and setting up the perfect amount of defenses: enough to deter pirates, but not so many as to make the Empires think that we were hiding something valuable there.

Val's position was largely a title without authority. I still felt unhappy about how I'd treated her when we'd been under Cubism, but I didn't really trust someone so young to make important decisions without clearing them with Marissa or me first.

The remaining members were Chris' team, which had grown to five, not including Chris himself. That was enough to keep round-the-clock surveillance on Cubism while still maintaining reasonable efforts to find the necessary items for the exploit ourselves. So far we'd had great success on that front with very little intervention from me. Chris' team would find something, then Marissa would send a squad to secure it. It was working without a hitch.

One Thursday, though, about three weeks after Artemis had launched, Chris had urgent news as soon as I logged in.

"Cubism is deploying. We think he's got a lock on one of the artifacts. Marissa's sent a scouting force, but we've been waiting on your command to send more."

My heart went from zero to a hundred in under a second. It was time to show Cubism what we were made of. "We're gonna send anyone who's online. We gotta teach Cubism who's in charge. Are Jeremy and Marissa both online?"

"Yep," Chris confirmed.

I hung up on Chris, desperate to get in touch with the others. I called Marissa first. "How many marines do you have ready to go?"

A pause. "Fourteen. But five of those are already en route to intercept."

"Mobilize the others. We want to hit Cubism has hard as possible."

"Roger," Marissa responded. I hung up on her and called Jeremy.

174

"You got another crew available to get nine more Marines to the site?"

"Damn right I do. Was just waiting for your command."

"Good. Get them going."

"Aye, aye, ma'am," Jeremy said, with a hint of irony in his voice. A reminder, perhaps, that my authority over him was arbitrary. Still, it seemed good natured enough and I put it out of my mind.

A few minutes later, I was crammed into a transport shuttle, one of our few ships, with the nine other marines that Marissa had ordered along. Val was ahead of us, leading the scouting team, and Jeremy was in our escort, a larger and more heavily armed ship flying a few clicks ahead. The result of this was that, despite my efforts to be friendly, I didn't really know anyone else that I was packed into the transport with.

Without a friend to chat to, the flight felt long and stressful. Logically, I knew that we hugely outnumbered Cubism's forces, but this logic didn't comfort me. He'd succeeded against the odds before.

"Five minutes out," called the pilot, whose name I couldn't recall. A few mumbled confirmations echoed from the marines. It occurred to me that my presence here might be bad for morale: might make the others feel like they were being evaluated. It was too late to turn back now, though.

"Two minutes. Scouting team has engaged the enemy. I'm putting you guys down on the other side of the hostiles, encircling them."

Another chorus of mumbling greeted the pilot's words.

We dropped out of lightspeed a moment later, the planet visible through the transport's few windows. The ship began to shake uncontrollably as we entered the atmosphere. I didn't know what the planet was called, I hadn't had time to check.

175

We'd elected not to use a planetcrash to get down to the surface, although Val's squad had. Cubism and his team didn't seem to have any anti-air capabilities, according to her initial reports, so it was safer just to land on the surface rather than fall.

Our transport touched down at the base of a hill that provided cover from any fire that might come from Cubism and whoever was behind him now.

"You three, around the right side of the hill: take position at that rock." I pointed out a boulder that seemed to be solid enough to provide decent cover. "You three, left side. I can't see any cover from here, keep pushing until you find something. Everyone else, straight up the hill with me. The trees won't be substantial enough for long term cover, but we'll hide there until we have a place to advance to. Let's move."

It took a couple more minutes to reach the summit of the hill. During that time, Val's team had been forced to hunker down, as they were taking a surprising amount of fire. Had Cubism expanded his team without us finding out? We didn't yet have a solid headcount of the hostile force...

As soon as we crested the hill, though, a hail of laser blasts came our way, cutting through the trees that we'd planned to use as camouflage. "Back down!" I shouted, before hitting the dirt and crawling away from the peak of the hill. Publius must be somewhere hidden above, watching us and reporting our positions to Cubism...damn! Why hadn't I thought of that?

Fortunately, my other combatants were able to advance. Cubism's gang could only put out enough fire to keep two of our squads suppressed at a time, so Val and I were forced to sit on our heels, taking fire as a distraction, while the two groups I'd sent flanking advanced.

After a minute though, a new ship, one I didn't recognize, rose from Cubism's position and into the air: they were pulling out. They jumped directly to lightspeed from the atmosphere: a risky move, but one that prevented Jeremy's crew from shooting them down.

Crap! How had this happened? I'd thought that Publius was watching us from above, but he was clearly on the ground...unless they had a second pilot and second ship now? It wasn't impossible. I hated the uncertainty. In the past I'd always been in a chain of command, and didn't need to worry about things like this. Now, though, I couldn't just pass questions up and forget about them.

I sighed. Time to see how complete our failure had been. "All squads, push forward to the cavern entrance to secure the area." The item Cubism had been pursuing, as far as Chris could determine, was an upgrade pack for a frigate, which would drop upon the death of the boss of the dungeon that was in a cavern here. The position that Cubism had taken up was just inside the cave and I could now see the reason why we hadn't noticed his escape ship until it was too late, the mouth of the cave was wide enough to hide a ship and make it invisible from the surface.

Val arrived at the cavern entrance a moment after I did.

"Hey Emily!" she called out, chipper as always. She brought a smile to my face even through the stress. "No way Cubism got the item. No. Way. We attacked him just a few seconds after he landed and everyone he had was forced to hold us off. No one was left to complete the dungeon, not in the amount of time before you forced them back. We did it!"

I wasn't so sure. "Let's double check that," I replied. "Take your team down into the caverns and get the upgrade kit for us. Only way to be sure."

"Roger that!" she said.

After thanking them for their prompt response and declaring the mission a success, I sent the rest of the marines back to base, but stayed outside the cavern to think about what had

177

happened. How had Cubism known our positions and been able to fire upon us as we crested the hill? Why had he been ready to pull out so quickly? We'd never had that kind of immediate exit strategy before: every mission had been all or nothing. Did he have some new recruit who was pushing him to change up his tactics? It was hard to say.

Eventually, though, Val's team resurfaced, and reported that they'd successfully cleared the cavern and returned with the upgrade kit. My stress melted away immediately. I'd been worried that Cubism had made it out one step closer to victory...Instead, we'd succeeded. We hadn't managed to kill Cubism and his team, as I'd hoped, but we were a step closer to activating the glitch before they could. If we could keep this up, we'd be there in no time. My questions about his change in tactics still nagged at me, but they were far less severe than when I'd thought they'd cost us an item. Now they only mattered looking forward, but I had plenty of time to figure it out. At least, I hoped I did...

I composed a short memo to all members of Artemis, congratulating them on their good work and the success of the mission, but reminding them that there was still much to be done. I hoped it would keep morale high enough that people would stick around. I'd worried that I might have scared some of them off with my presence on the mission. It wasn't typical for faction leaders to go on every mission, even critically important ones, but I didn't want to just watch from the sidelines.

Shortly after I sent that out, I got a reply from Jeremy.

```
nice work on the note to the troops. you
seemed pretty tense, though, you gotta chill
out. tell you what, youre living near andrew
square, right? drop by my place this evening
```

His street address was below. A strange mix of emotions hit me. All of the worst-case scenarios from "stranger danger" classes rushed back to me, but so did an excitement at the prospect of seeing Jeremy in person. I'd only known him for a few weeks, but we'd grown close in that time, closer than I'd ever been to anyone I'd known IRL. I couldn't just pass this up, could I? But my wariness remained, in conflict with my desire for a real companion.

Eventually eagerness won out, but wariness demanded a concession.

```
sounds good, but id rather we meet somewhere
public. can you catch me in front of the BPL?
its where i come to play planetcrash, so im
already here
```

His response came far quicker than mine did to him:

```
no problem. ill let you know as soon as im
there.
```

He signaled his arrival a little under half an hour later, and I logged out of *PlanetCrash* to go down and meet him.

CHAPTER 29

I walked onto the front steps of the BPL, my nerves rivaling how I'd felt when I ran away from home. Glancing over the wide stairs and beyond to the green across the street, no one immediately stood out to me as Jeremy. I'd never seen him before, of course, but until now I'd had a feeling that I would just instantly recognize him…apparently not. I sat down and looked over the crowd again. The move wasn't in order rest: I'd been sitting for hours before in *PlanetCrash*. But unable to pick Jeremy out of a crowd, I tried to make myself look like I was waiting for someone, hoping that would tip him off to who I was.

Sure enough, a minute or two later, a boy about my age approached. He was quite a bit taller than I, probably a bit above average. He smiled as he saw me, a genuine grin that reached his eyes, and I figured this must be Jeremy.

"Emily?" Jeremy asked, confirming that it was him.

"Yeah," I replied. A lot of people used their real names for their *PlanetCrash* characters, but a lot didn't. Neither was considered odd. "Is Jeremy good for you?"

"Absolutely."

I stood up. "Did you have anything you wanted to do while we're here? Or should we just head back."

He chuckled. "Hey, I wanted to meet in Southie. You're the one who dragged me out here."

180

It was true. And now that he was standing here in front of me, it seemed like it had been a needless precaution. I winced. "Sorry about that. I was just nervous—I've never met anyone from *PlanetCrash* in real life before."

"Me either...never really gotten close with anyone before."

Although my heart leapt in warmth for him, I wasn't sure how to respond to that, so I just changed the subject. "How are we getting back to Southie? Green Line or Orange?" The Green Line would undoubtedly be faster, its nearest station, Copley, was less than a hundred meters away, while the Orange Lines' Back Bay station was a couple minutes' walk. But the Green Line was one of the last remaining rapid transit lines in Boston that hadn't been upgraded to a monorail and instead remained with the same light rail system that it had been since its opening over a century ago. It made for a much less pleasant experience: with jerky motion, shrieking brakes, and it was a lot more crowded since it served so many destinations.

"Green," Jeremy replied. "I hate walking."

About half an hour later, we disembarked in Andrew Square. The SHU was visible from the station, of course, but I tried not to look at it. I didn't want to think about that half of my life right now. Jeremy didn't mention it, thankfully, and we proceeded up Dorchester Ave talking cheerfully about the mission from earlier, each playfully exaggerating our contributions. We both knew that Val and her team had done most of the real legwork, but it was fun to brag, especially when the other person knew you were full of it.

It was only a few minutes more before we arrived at Jeremy's house, an old triple-decker, one of the last remaining in the city.

"I live alone here," Jeremy said. "After my dad died, I did my best to slip through the cracks. My mom hadn't been around for years before that, but dad had never removed her

181

from bills or the deed or paperwork or anything: he was still in denial, hoping she might come back. Now I just impersonate her so that I don't get thrown into foster care...once I'm eighteen, though, I'll try to get her declared dead as well."

"How do you pay the bills?" I asked, astonished.

"Dad had life insurance. Should be enough to last until I'm eighteen. Other than that, though, I had been hoping that Cubism would pay out big for me...that's impossible now, so I guess I should get back to looking at jobs." His voice had hardened as we spoke, losing the light tone it had held before. It hurt to be confronted with this, the reality of what leaving Cubism had meant to Jeremy.

It meant the same to me, of course, but at least I had a family to go back to when all this was over...if they didn't kill me when I returned.

The mood had significantly darkened by the time we reached his kitchen, especially considering that we were supposed to be celebrating. Jeremy had noticed it too. "We gotta lighten up," he said. "Gimme a sec." He headed into a different room, leaving me behind in the kitchen where we'd come it. I took a look around. It was surprisingly neat and tidy. I wouldn't have expected a sixteen-year-old boy living alone to keep up with cleaning, but Jeremy evidently did. There wasn't much on the countertops, either in the way of crumbs, dust, or dirty dishes. There was a short stack of clean pots by the sink, presumably from some recent meal, and a tea kettle sat on the stove, its aluminum unblemished. I stole a peek into his fridge as well, curious about what he was eating. Inside was a half gallon carton of milk, a partially empty jar of marinara sauce, a carton of eggs and a drawer with a few bags of lettuce. Presumably there were boxes of pasta somewhere else. I shut the door before sitting up on the counter to wait for Jeremy to return.

He did a few seconds later, holding a bottle.

182

"Kentucky straight bourbon whiskey," he announced. "Let's go."

"Where'd you get that?" I asked, even though I could guess the answer.

"Dad bought it. Want some?"

I considered it. I'd never had alcohol, not outside of the watered-down wine they gave us at Mass on Sundays. But surely one drink couldn't hurt, could it? I nodded and Jeremy grabbed two glasses, pouring the whiskey into each. It seemed like a lot, but perhaps that was just my inexperience judging the glass.

We clinked glasses and drank down the amber liquid. I'd expected the whiskey to taste somewhat similar to the communal wine, but stronger. Not at all. It burned my mouth and throat as it went down. I shuddered involuntarily from the unfamiliar taste and sensation the whiskey gave. Once I swallowed, though, it sat in my stomach and filled me with warmth.

As we continued to talk, I loosened. It felt like relaxing muscles I'd been holding tensed my entire life without knowing. Soon a strange pressure hummed against my skull, an odd but pleasant sensation.

Before I knew what was happening, he'd refilled my glass and I'd downed that as well...and again. And soon after that, I blacked out.

183

CHAPTER 30

I woke up back in the SHU with a throbbing headache, and blinded by the sun streaming through my room's only window and directly into my eyes. My thoughts were sluggish, more so than they usually were in the morning. A hangover? I supposed it must be...how much had I had?

God, I couldn't remember nearly anything and what time was it? The sun didn't usually shine in my eyes in the morning...

I checked my phone but the battery was dead. Rolling off the mattress that sat on the floor to grope around for my charger, I found myself having trouble getting my hand to do what I expected it to. Everything was just...a little off, like when you got server lag in a video game.

After struggling with my poor coordination for a bit, I managed to get my phone plugged into its charger via the adapter in the wall. Then I collapsed back to my mattress as I waited for it to charge up a bit. God, who knew that alcohol was so strong?

I let my mind wander for a few minutes, daydreaming about returning home once I'd finished my mission here. It was the first time I'd felt homesick, really, and probably was just a lingering effect of the alcohol. But I did miss my parents. Knowing Jeremy and Ezra's situations, even what was happening with Cubism...it made me feel extremely lucky that my parents were only out of touch with me, and not far, far worse: the situations the others had to deal with. Even the pressure from Val's parents was crushing and overwhelming compared to what my parents expected of me.

I wished, momentarily, that I'd listened and never left home, but shook that off as idle sentimentalism. Without me, Cubism would be able to pull of the heist of a lifetime unchecked, potentially upending the lives of the tens of thousands of innocent people on *PlanetCrash*'s NA-22 server. It was unacceptable. And I had to stop it.

A few minutes later I rolled over again, to check my phone, which probably had enough charge to be serviceable for a while now. I powered it on and was shocked by the time when the lock screen booted: 3:22 PM? How long had I slept! What time had I gone to bed? It was incredibly disconcerting that I couldn't remember the answer to either question.

A thought struck me, a bolt from the blue: I'd missed more than half of the library's hours for the day. By the time I got there, it'd be at least four, only five hours from closing. I sprung to my feet, nearly tripping as a sudden wave of dizziness and nausea rushed over me. I forced myself to stabilize and keep moving. After throwing on the first clothes I could find in my room, I fled my room towards the monorail with an unsteady sprint.

I calmed down once I was on the train inbound towards the central library. Yeah, I'd lost some time, but it wouldn't be the end of the world. Honestly, I'd needed the break anyway…months on end of twelve-hour days in *PlanetCrash* had been exhausting and had stripped all of the fun I'd previously had out of the game. Probably, I should take breaks like this more often: though next time I'd have to let my officers know ahead of time, so that I didn't leave them in the lurch…they could handle it though; I trusted them. That said, I didn't know

185

if Jeremy was up and moving yet. Doubtless he'd had as much to drink as I had, if not more.

As expected, I arrived at the library shortly after four p.m. I jogged up the stairs feeling the same uncoordinated lagginess that I had in my bedroom. It wouldn't be a good day for anything requiring mechanical skills from me. *Maybe I shouldn't have come in at all,* I thought as I logged in to *PlanetCrash. Taken the whole day off.* But since I was already here, I should at least check in with Artemis to see how things were going.

Discord had almost finished downloading when *Planet-Crash* finished booting up and spawned me back at Artemis HQ.

...no, it must have spawned me somewhere else. A glitch, perhaps? Instead of the hangar where I'd despawned, bustling with Artemis personnel, ships, and equipment, I was in some kind of abandoned warehouse. Small fires burned around me, eating away what little structure remained.

I had to leave before the building collapsed on me: I didn't know that my character could survive that level of blunt and burning damage. I dashed for the nearest exit I could see, a hole in a wall from an area where the fires had already burned out and caused a small collapse. After vaulting through and out of the warehouse, I continued on for a few meters more to get clear of the building.

Now that I was momentarily safe, I looked around and tried to get my bearings. The mountainous forest, with trees as tall as the peaks, was immediately familiar: I was still on the same planet as Artemis HQ, at least.

A crash from behind caused me to spin around in time to see another piece of the warehouse fall into itself, but something far more chilling distracted me. From the outside, now I could see it: the shape of the building, the logo at the center of the wall...this was our headquarters. While I'd been drinking and

186

celebrating with Jeremy, someone had found it and destroyed everything.

These enemies could still be nearby, so I dashed over to the nearby foliage and went prone.

Once in cover, though, the reality of the situation caught up to me and I could barely restrain myself from a cacophony of cursing that would surely have gotten me kicked out of—perhaps even banned from—the library.

I alt-tabbed over to the Discord server, which had loaded while I'd been in *PlanetCrash*. The voice chat was packed: half of the alliance must have been there. I connected to a hidden channel that only officers could see, then pinged Marissa to join me.

"Where the hell have you been!" She snapped at me as she entered.

"I'm sorry," I replied. "I needed a break. I didn't know this would happen."

She sighed, seeming to let go of some of her anger. "How much do you know?"

"Just that I'm hiding in a bush outside the burned husk of our base."

"I guess there's a lot to cover, then. This morning, a group of the most powerful factions on the server announced that they'd decided to form an alliance: supposedly to eliminate pirates and griefers throughout the server. They're calling themselves the Skydrifter Union. Each faction leader sits on their 'high council' and the council elects a chair. Three guesses who they picked."

"Cubism."

"Yup. I don't know how he got them to do this, but their first action as an alliance was to label Artemis as 'griefers' and take out our headquarters. I'm sure Cubism will fight actual griefers, to keep up appearances, but he's got some powerful friends now."

"I'm guessing he offered them shares of the cash," I replied. "Probably isn't hard to get someone to give up control of their *PlanetCrash* faction for a million IRL."

"Probably not. But that's a lot of people—if that's what he did, he's really starting to dilute the shares. More than fifty factions joined the alliance. He can't possibly have promised them all equal benefit."

"Hmm. I guess he has some other tricks up his sleeve."

"There is some good news, though," Marissa said. "Cubism was too obvious about his attack on us. It's brought a lot of attention to Artemis and to your post explaining that Cubism is planning to rob them all blind."

"I guess we can try to rebuild?" I said, hesitantly. "But we'll have to be a lot stronger on information security this time."

A chill went through me as I thought about the question that Marissa hadn't addressed. "How did they know where to find us? No one knew unless they'd been here."

"I only see one possibility..." Marissa began, but I'd already realized it.

"Cubism has a mole inside Artemis." I finished Marissa's sentence for her.

She simply grunted in agreement.

"Until we figure out a way to root out the mole, don't let people regroup. We've gotta stay scattered so that they can't just strike again."

"I'll pass the order along," Marissa said. She paused. "Do you have any ideas about the mole?"

"Not yet, unfortunately...I'll let you know if I come up with anything, though."

"Okay. I'll start spreading the word to stay apart. Talk to you later?"

"Gotcha. Bye."

"Bye." She disconnected from the call.

It was time to get off-planet. There would be nothing left for me here.

CHAPTER 31

When Marissa had said that the attack had brought a lot of attention to Artemis, I'd thought she was simply trying to buck me up, keep me from giving up. But over the next days and weeks, it became clear that the opposite was true, she'd been underselling the situation. Cubism had been smart to keep his team low-key initially and had vastly overreacted when we'd cornered him. His new "alliance" was larger than any empire I'd ever seen in *PlanetCrash* before. And it had formed suddenly. Instead of the years that many empires spent grinding tiny increases in their strength to get to half that size, the Skydrifter Union had formed overnight. This rapid growth had panicked the leaders of every major faction that hadn't been invited. So I wasn't too surprised when I received communication from Gideon, leader of the Tannhauser Gate Alliance, the largest faction that wasn't part of the Union, looking to join with us. He'd seen how Artemis had been targeted and saw us as natural allies against the Skydrifters.

"I don't know why the Skydrifter Union targeted you," he'd said, "but working together is the only way either of us will be able to survive long."

I wholeheartedly agreed.

After some well-intentioned negotiation and discussion, we decided that the best way to run our alliance was for Tannhauser Gate—and any other factions that might join us in the future—to act largely autonomously, still lead by Gideon. He would take his directives from me, then implement them as he saw best, using his superior knowledge of his own troops and systems.

Soon after we announced our agreement, other factions Cubism hadn't bribed began to follow Gideon's lead and asked to join Artemis as subfactions on similar terms. Of course, I was delighted to accept them.

Less than a month after Artemis' near destruction, we were nearly as large as the Skydrifter Union. Cubism had polarized near the entire NA-22 server.

Once the Skydrifters realized that the rest of the server was uniting against them, they'd deployed as fast as they could, occupying every planet they could get their hands on without much thought of what value each might have. It took longer to decide if something was worthwhile than it did to capture it, so why wait for a decision?

They had a head start, as I'd spent a lot of time trying to get Artemis organized before we were able to start making our own moves. But once we got rolling, we were able to seize a great deal of our own territory. Besides which, the Skydrifters eventually limited themselves to just over a quarter of the planets on NA-22. Marissa guessed that this was the greatest area over which they could actually project force while still maintaining enough reserves to respond rapidly to any threats. All of the intelligence Chris had managed to get so far agreed, but we remained wary in case Cubism was holding another reserve in hiding from us.

As for Artemis, I'd put each of my core four officers, Val, Chris, Marissa, and Jeremy, in charge of one area of our operations. Chris, of course, was our spymaster, responsible for what I now officially christened the Artemis Directorate of Intelligence. Jeremy was the lead of our Navy, the segment of Artemis troops that stayed mobile, patrolled, and engaged the Skydrifters directly when necessary. Marissa, on the other hand, lead the marines, charged with defending the solid ground of the planets we already held.

Val's youth kept me from placing her in a role that required that level of logistical depth, but she had proven apt in the tactics of an immediate fight. With this in mind, I'd put her in charge of our Special Operations: a small team that I planned to use whenever Chris found one of the necessary items for the glitch. Val would lead them in to secure whatever item it was, even if it was deep in Skydrifter territory. That assumed, of course, that Chris would be able to get his hands on that kind of information. All in all, I felt that it was as good of a system as I could reasonably have asked for, especially given the ludicrously short time we had to put it together. Entire factions that had volunteered to join Artemis had been unceremoniously thrown into one of the three main departments, with a few of their most skilled players joining SpecOps.

The galaxy was now split in two. Only a handful of minor factions had declined to throw their lot in with either me or Cubism and between us we now controlled over half the galaxy. The remainder made up the dense galactic core, where planets and stars were far closer together, making it near impossible to hold as a large empire like ours. It was too easy, there, for a small group of insurgents to hide from our large, unwieldy war machines. Losses would be calamitous. Cubism and I knew this: neither of us even attempted to hold that area. Internally at Artemis, we'd codenamed it The Mosh Pit, at Marissa's suggestion.

Since The Mosh Pit's high density of planets meant a greater likelihood that the necessary items would spawn there, even after accounting for the fact that the further flung planets tended to get better loot drops, I had Chris keeping up a constant presence of spies throughout the galactic core, hopping from planet

192

to planet, talking to NPCs, trying to chase down the locations of the key items. For information security, Chris made sure that no one spy had the full key item list, or even a significant fragment. It meant that we were probably missing out on some valuable pickups, but I was still worried about information security following the leak of Artemis Headquarters to Cubism. Sure, he already had the list himself, but the last thing I needed was another group working on the exploit without us knowing. Whenever Chris' team found something, Val would lead in a strike group to secure it. It was a clean, efficient operation.

Jeremy and Marissa, on the other hand, lead a logistical nightmare. To integrate the soldiers of dozens of armies into a single cohesive unit would take an immense amount of work. We were far from combat ready as we stood: our navy was just a patchwork collection of ships brought by the factions that had joined Artemis, with far too many corvettes and subcapital ships compared to the relatively few cruisers and dreadnoughts, which only a select group of factions could afford. Jeremy had people working round the clock on scavenging resources from our territory and building them into new capital ships that could hold the line of battle against Cubism's forces. He'd designated the first dreadnought we put under construction as my flagship, which I named the A.S.V. *Boston*, both as a point of vanity for myself and as a recognition of Jeremy.

We built a few more dreadnoughts, knowing they'd be critical in any decisive engagement against the Skydrifters, but soon shifted down to the small ships that were more efficient for the resources required, especially when most battles would likely be smaller skirmishes than massive battles like the one between the Ceruleans and United Front that I remembered all too well from my previous character's death. A dreadnought took long enough to mobilize that you could lose precious time trying to bring one to an engagement that didn't merit its firepower, po-

193

tentially allowing the enemy to get in and out before you arrived.

Because of this, we focused on smaller, faster ships, especially corvettes and transports. Most of our fights would likely be quick battles as we raced to secure items in the Mosh Pit, so the investment into the speed of our ships could pay huge dividends.

Marissa had a less severe deficit of infrastructure in her marines than Jeremy did in the Navy, so her time was mostly spent organizing massive training exercises. Not only were these a great source of practice for our marines, but they also kept everyone entertained and happy. *PlanetCrash* was a video game, at the end of the day, and I didn't know how many of our troops actually believed me when I'd told them that their money was in danger. So I thought it a good policy to make a reasonable effort to make sure people were having fun, though never at the cost of tangible disadvantages.

All in all, it was an incredible operation, the second biggest empire in *PlanetCrash*'s history. We only fell short to the one that mattered most: Cubism's.

CHAPTER 32

It was just over two months into the war with the Skydrifters that I found myself back on the Summer Street Bridge with Ezra again. It was near fall now, and the weather had cooled off enough that it was pleasant to be outdoors. The sun set at our backs as we sat on the edge of the bridge, staring out into the Atlantic. We hadn't said much, instead just sitting quietly and enjoying each other's presence.

Honestly, I was glad that Ezra was happy to sit quietly. I was so burned out from running Artemis that my brain was fried badly enough that even a simple conversation with a good friend seemed exhausting. Being in charge was a full-time job. Actually, it was more than that: Erza had a full-time job and came out of it both with more free time than I had. Plus he got paid...

For the first weeks, I'd just continued putting full days in at the library, like I had before, but eventually I'd started taking Artemis back to the SHU with me. Since most of my job was administrative and strategic, I could do it from my phone without even being logged into *PlanetCrash*. Now there was barely any justification for me to go into the library at all, except when I needed to pick up an item, since I kept all of the key items in my personal inventory. It also meant I wasn't levelling up as fast as I had been before. I was still at level 32, with that level 26 autoshotgun I'd purchased largely unused. But since I wasn't leading ground troops, I didn't seem so important to keep my

195

personal stats up. Other than picking up items, though, I wasn't needed in the game, I was needed to meet with each member of my key leadership team daily to get updates on each aspect of Artemis, and to pass down orders. It would have been more time-efficient to meet with them all together, but continued evidence of leaks to Cubism's spies kept me paranoid to the point of hiding intelligence from Marissa and orders from Chris. Val I also had on a need-to-know basis, not because I thought she might be a traitor but because I worried she'd accidentally let something to slip to someone who was. That left Jeremy as the only other person in Artemis who I could trust with everything.

I sighed aloud. He'd been the one who convinced me I needed to take a day off, disconnect from *PlanetCrash* and reset. And yet here I was, thinking about it anyway, not even taking the opportunity to talk to Erza.

"I'm sorry," I said, turning to Ezra. He snorted, not looking away from the ocean in its twilight.

"Don't apologize to me. The only person you're hurting is yourself."

"You were right," I said. "I should never have gotten involved with all this."

Now he looked towards me, and I saw a powerful emotion in his eyes that I couldn't quite place. "You can still leave."

"And let Cubism just get away with it?"

"Not necessarily. You've already built an opposition. Just turn it over to Jeremy—that's his name, right?—and let him run that while you put your life back together."

It was sorely tempting. I knew already that I'd have to go back to my old life eventually, since I wasn't going to be walking away from this a millionaire and every day I didn't the consequences simply built up further. "I don't know...it would take time to transition things over to him..."

196

"You guys can afford a couple days off of peak performance, can't you?"

"We really can't." I took a deep breath, breaking eye contact to look back towards the twilight. "We're losing. It's hard to say exactly how far along Cubism is, since our intel isn't perfect, but as far as we can say, the next item that he finds could be the last. Any downtime is a huge risk. Even my being here is a luxury we can barely afford."

"It's not a luxury; it's a necessity. You need time to cool down."

"I know. I'm here, aren't I? But it still worries me."

A moment of silence passed before Erza spoke again. "How far away are you? I mean, how many more items do you need?"

"One or two. Depends how you count, I guess."

"What's that mean?" He seemed genuinely curious.

"The last two are Kai and Asha: a pair of ultra-rare, legendary swords with linked spawning. So when one appears, its sister will drop elsewhere on the planet. Finding one basically guarantees finding both."

"And Cubism? Does he have a set of them yet?"

"If he does, we're screwed," I replied bluntly. "Those are the rarest drop on the entire list. It could be months before either of us get them. Or it could be tomorrow. Which is why I can't let my guard down."

He frowned. "I guess you've given this a lot of thought already, haven't you."

It wasn't a question, but I nodded nonetheless, and we lapsed back into silence.

That was the end of our *PlanetCrash* discussion for the night, and I was finally, finally able to get my mind off the conflict, if only for a few fleeting hours. I slept far easier that night than I had for quite some time.

197

CHAPTER 33

As it happened, it was only a week and a half later that I received a phone call from Chris shortly after I woke up.

"This is it!" he nearly shouted, and I immediately knew he meant Kai or Asha.

"Where?"

"The Skydrifters have Asha in one of their warehouses. On a small planet, near the edge of their territory."

"And Kai?" I asked.

"As far as we can tell, they've got teams still scouring the planet for it."

"Then we don't have a lot of time. Call the others. Tell Marissa and Jeremy to muster the entire faction. It's showtime. I'll meet you when I'm back in-game."

The monorail ride back to the library was agonizingly slow and felt longer than it ever had before. Months of work building Artemis into an effective fighting force was about to be tested. And while every second counted, I still thought it would be smarter to make sure we knew what we were doing before taking action. To look before we leapt into battle, as it were. So Jeremy, Val, Marissa, Chris, and I got into a Discord call together to discuss our plan.

Chris started by briefing us. "One of my guys found Kai as it was being transported to a warehouse on Carthas, a small planet on the edge of Skydrifer territory. As I'm sure you all

198

remember, the linked spawning of Asha means that the sword has to be elsewhere on the surface of Carthas. And given that there's been no change in my financials as of late, we can assume Cubism hasn't found it yet either."

"So we need to take the planet for long enough to find Asha?" Marissa asked.

"That's how I see it," I replied. "Marissa, Jeremy: how many of your people are available right now?"

"I've got five hundred and twenty-one reporting in," Marissa replied promptly.

"Just shy of eight hundred," was Jeremy's response. "We're lucky it's a Saturday."

"And Val? How much of your team is here?"

"Eight of us, not including me."

"Okay," I began. "Here's what I'm thinking. Val and her team go in first to secure the warehouse and find Kai. Once they have first contact with the Skydrifters, we'll drop the whole navy out of lightspeed and station into orbit around Carthas. Marissa, we'll land your five hundred and immediately start on getting them set up defensively. But take about a hundred to start searching any likely lootable areas." It was lucky planets in *PlanetCrash* were so much smaller than in our real galaxy, or this search would have dragged on much longer. A hundred players could probably loot the whole planet within the day.

"Do you want my people in the ground, too?" Chris asked. "We did spec for this kind of fight, but the extra bodies couldn't hurt."

"No. I need you to tell me how soon and how hard the Skydrifters can strike back. It might give us a better chance to prepare."

199

"Let's move, then," Jeremy said, with an unusual quaver in his voice. Likely from the nerves. "We know what we have to do and the sooner we start the better."

"I couldn't agree more," I replied. "Let's get everyone to their battle stations."

When I was finally able to log in, I took the helm of the *Boston*, of course, which was no longer the largest dreadnought in the Artemis fleet, but still remained my flagship. Jeremy usually had it under his direct command, but today he'd be taking the A.S.V. *Los Angeles* instead: which was our largest.

As our navy jumped to lightspeed to position just out of Carthas' sensor range, I couldn't help but feel that I should have made some rousing speech to the troops of Artemis, something to build morale for the coming battle. Nothing came to mind, however, and enthusing people had never been my strong suit anyway. I decided to let the flight pass in silence, letting the line chat amongst themselves instead.

All our ships save for Val's dropped from lightspeed at the designated position and we hung in the black expanse. Her small transport raced forward onto battle. It was only about a minute further to Carthas.

Val, along with quite a few other of our more elite operatives, was wearing a small transponder which would allow me to see through her eyes. Those transponders were valuable pieces of loot which we'd recovered as we'd scoured the galaxy for the items necessary to complete our quest.

I booted hers up and suddenly it seemed as though I was aboard the A.S.V. *Blackwing*, Val's stealth transport. Of course I was actually still on the *Boston*, and could jump back immediately if the need required.

"Fifteen seconds to drop!" Val called out. "Lock and load." Her team didn't react, having been locked and loaded since before they'd even boarded the *Blackwing*. That was just how *PlanetCrash* marines were.

"Prep for drop." her next command came a few seconds later. Each member of her team stepped cleanly into their planetcrash pods, ready to be shot at the surface with devastating speed. A moment later, Val followed and her own pod door sealed behind her. *The Blackwing* dropped from lightspeed directly into orbit of Carthas and fired its elite payload with a series of flashes of blinding light.

Again, Val was the last to go, that was her responsibility as the commanding officer of the mission. Through the porthole in her pod I could see the other eight below her, each trailing an exhaust from the thrusters that propelled them groundward faster than Carthas' gravity alone could manage. One by one they disappeared into the clouds, and Val followed. Then came a split second of darkness before we emerged into a deluge of rain below. The landing retro-thrusters fired almost immediately after, slowing our descent so that the pod wouldn't explode on impact.

That's not to say the landing was gentle. I could see the violent splashes of mud and exhaust gases below as the others were driven into the ground. When Val hit, I could have sworn I was on board and I felt the primal surge of pre-combat adrenaline, my brain failing to process that I wasn't even in control.

The shooting had already started by the time Val had scrambled out of her pod; the warehouse guards, having heard the blasts of the pods impact with the ground, were experienced enough players to know instantly what that sound implied.

Back on the *Boston*, I signaled to my First Officer to have Jeremy give the engage order to the fleet. I pulled myself out of Val-vision only for a moment, though, before jumping back in. My crew would notify me when Skydrifter reinforcements arrived from the stars.

Looking back into Val's perspective, I could see that the guards had pulled back into the warehouse for better cover, leaving a slumped soggy corpse on the ramparts atop the roof. Val was dishing out orders to her troops on how to proceed: "Goobs, Meritt, Ike, and Penny," she said, addressing them by their in-game tags, "Scale up the side and go in from the top: there's gotta be an entrance up there that they pulled back into. The rest of you, let's try to blow the front door. Move!"

They snapped into action, the soldiers that she'd called out using various means to get up to the roof based on the loot they'd collected. Goobs deployed a jetpack to shoot herself up to the top, Meritt had gloves and boots with spikes that made climbing far easier, Penny had a grappling hook, and Ike…well, Ike hitched a ride with Goobs.

Back on the ground, Val lead the remaining four of her command in setting up shaped charges around the frame of the main entrance. The squad took cover around the sides of the warehouse before detonating the charges. A rapid series of explosions obliterated the wall they'd targeted: they'd used way more explosives than necessary. I could only hope no damage had been done to the sword inside.

As Val and the others filed in through the gaping hole they'd created, I was pinged back to the *Boston's* main deck.

"Marissa's reporting that she's beginning to land our marines on the surface," an officer I didn't recognize gave the report. "If you'd like to oversee."

"Thank you," I replied. "Dismissed." I considered my options. Val's team was in the more immediately interesting situation, but Marissa's deployment was more likely to determine the final outcome of the battle. I swapped over to viewing Marissa's transponder.

In the reverse of the tradition for squads in *PlanetCrash* pods, Marissa's shuttle would be the first to touch down. It was

202

still in the process of landing as my vision merged with Marissa's, but the twenty-four marines who were onboard with her had already begun to jump out, taking up defensive positions around the perimeter. More shuttles were descending around them, twenty-seven in total, carrying not only Marissa's five hundred and twenty-one troops but also heavier weapons than infantry could carry: structural materials for fortifications, and a few smaller vehicles for ground transportation. Jeremy had sent down a squadron of fighter ships as well, presumably to ensure air superiority in case any of the Skydrifters got past his orbital defenses. They flew overhead in a tight formation, low enough that the grass rippled as they passed.

I took a moment to marvel at the detail of *PlanetCrash*, the processing power that must have gone into each droplet of rain and blade of grass on each planet throughout the entire galaxy that PlanetCrash Studios had built.

Marissa pulled me back into the moment as her second-in-command, Auriel, came over to her, having landed on another transport shuttle.

"I'm liking this location as much on the ground as I did from orbit," Auriel shouted to be heard over the torrential rain.

"Yeah," Marissa called back. "I don't think we'll need to relocate. Tell the builders to get to work: I want this place impenetrable in fifteen." It was an unreasonable goal, but you gave those sometimes and it did no more harm than a coach asking for a hundred-and-ten per cent effort. "Did you send out the search team yet?"

Auriel nodded. "They're on the hunt for Asha."

"Tell them to let us know if they see signs of any Skydrifter forces remaining on-planet. We haven't gotten a fix on any other than the warehouse guards yet, which is making me nervous as all hell."

"Will do. Do we want a designated team for that?"

"Nah," Marissa replied. "The navy's got some birds on the hunt. Do send a platoon over to the warehouse to help the SpecOps team hold it, though."

So that was why the fighters had been flying so low. A clever move on Jeremy's part, assuming they could see anything with how fast they were flying.

Marissa dismissed Auriel, who saluted and left to execute her orders. The landing site, now officially Marissa's base of operations on the surface of Carthas, was bustling with activity. The order to reinforce the position came through from Auriel in mere moments and the marines who Marrisa had assigned specifically to the construction jumped into action now that it was confirmed they wouldn't have to move from the landing site. Above us, pre-fab buildings were fired down from the navy with pinpoint accuracy onto locations that we were marking on the ground, while simultaneously the fortifications we'd brought down went up around the perimeter. They were primarily to hold off a ground assault, but we had a couple anti-aircraft cannons to prevent airstrikes. Those couldn't stop a planetcrash, though. It was Jeremy's job to prevent the Skydrifters from getting into the correct orbital position to launch one, a position which I was currently holding with the *Boston*.

I was pinged once again that I was needed on deck, so I let my view of Carthas fade and the bridge return.

"We're starting to pick up Skydrifter vessels on our sensors," was the report I got. "About two minutes out from combat distance."

"What?" I nearly shouted. "Already? How'd they..." I cursed. "Battle stations! And get me Chris, *now*."

I took a few deep breaths while I waited for Chris to arrive, calming myself down. Likely this was just a small force that happened to be in the area. The guards at the warehouse had seen under a dozen attackers, and probably called for help without

204

realizing the larger force of marines landing nearby. Neverthe-less, I should check in with Chris anyway, in case he had an idea of when the main fleet would be arriving. My heart rate slowly settled back down to normal.

Looking out the reinforced glass that separated the bridge from the blackness, I gazed at the stars, waiting for the fight to start.

The first Skydrifter ship seemed to materialize in the dis-tance as it dropped from lightspeed. A dreadnought. The most dangerous of any class of ship in *PlanetCrash*. In a way it was fortunate: one less to fight when the main fleet arrived. We outnumbered it six to one.

But then a second dreadnought appeared. A third...then smaller ships came as well, cruisers and artillery, corvettes and destroyers. Soon Skydrifter ships appeared faster than I could keep track of their class. I could spot at least one carrier unload-ing fighters, though, and a group of corvettes jumping out ahead of the pack to start scouting us out.

Our own fighters began to fly through my view to engage the Skydrifters' before they reached the capital ships, closely fol-lowed by our own corvettes. Coming from behind them, an enormous laser blast sliced through the darkness towards the Skydrifter fleet. It was a shot from the main gun of the *Los An-geles*, Jeremy had reacted quickly. Perhaps a bit too quickly, as his shot missed, but it reminded me that I was neglecting my own duties.

I turned to my first officer. "Start diverting power to charg-ing up our main gun. And until we suffer damage, get the repair crews onto our light weapons instead of the autotargeting."

"Aye," he replied, and dashed off to execute my orders. I grabbed the control for the *Boston*'s main gun, and a reticle was projected into my vision. After taking a moment to line up a shot at one of the leading Skydrifter corvettes, I fired. The entire enemy ship shuddered with the force of my shot and our propellant level dipped almost imperceptibly as the thrusters compensated for the kick and vibrations. The lance of light was emitted after a moment, smashing into corvette I'd been aiming for and blowing a hole straight through its hull. I zoomed the *Boston*'s sensors in for a closer view and could see that the bridge had been blown wide open. That ship would no longer be a threat.

It would take a few minutes for the main canon to re-charge: longer if we used power for other purposes, like ma-neuvering or buffing our shielding. I'd wait until the last possi-ble second before diverting power away from the main gun, though. That was why the Skydrifter dreadnoughts wouldn't return our fire, yet, they had to move in and get closer.

Around me, our other four dreadnoughts (*New York*, *Chi-cago*, *San Francisco*, and *Atlanta*) opened fire as well, two of their shots connecting with targets deeper into the Skydrifter fleet than the corvette I'd blasted. It was a smart strategy: forcing the enemy ships to keep their power focused on forward shield-ing would divert energy away from either their propulsion or their armament. Either one would buy us time, something that became more precious with every mile the Skydrifters crossed in their approach.

Up ahead, the two opposing groups of fighters reached each other and engaged, melting from the organized formations of their charge into a chaotic mess of dogfights. The *Los Angeles* fired again, destroying another Skydrifter corvette. I was amazed at how quickly the turnaround had been. I'd known that the *LA* had the greatest power generation of any ship in our fleet, but the charge time was still remarkable, the *Boston*'s gun was still less than halfway ready. Jeremy must have been diverting power away from everything to get the guns up as soon as possible. It was risky, as he might not be able to get his shields back up to strength if he left this too long, but for now it seemed to be paying off.

A volley of fire came from the Skydrifters' artillery ships. Their guns were nearly as powerful as a dreadnought's, but they lacked the armor and defenses necessary to protect themselves. We hadn't invested in any artillery ships of our own: they weren't what you wanted when you had the smaller fleet. One shot impacted the *Boston*'s shields, dropping their strength to half. I grimaced and diverted some power off of charging our canon and onto keeping the shields up. It brought our charge rate down to an interminable crawl.

The Skydrifter main fleet continued to draw ever closer. As it neared the intricate entanglement of dogfights between our fighters and theirs, I gave the order that ours fall back. They had done their job of preventing the enemy from disrupting our corvettes from scouting and staying around any longer was suicide. At the same time, I received the scouting report from our corvettes. The Skydrifters had ten dreadnoughts, two cruisers, eighteen frigates, twelve destroyers, five corvettes (well, three now that we'd disabled two), six artillery, thirty transports, and a single carrier. It was, all told, a shockingly large fleet. How had they gotten it here so quickly? Had they been running training exercises nearby?

Regardless, we were badly outgunned. There was little hope we could win this fight: the goal was to delay them long enough for Marissa's troops to locate Asha. Then I'd drop down to the planet's surface and trigger the glitch. Assuming we could hold them off.

The one spark of hope I had was that they didn't seem to have too many transports, so it was unlikely that they had a much higher population of marines than we did. The battle on the ground might be winnable, assuming that the Skydrifters cared enough about getting Kai and Asha enough to hold back from carpet bombing the entire planet from orbit. And if they didn't…well, then everything might go back to how it had been a few days ago, but with both our fleets considerably lighter in tonnage.

I considered ordering the other battleships to concentrate fire on the transports, but rejected the idea. They'd be hard to hit, as they were sitting behind the other Skydrifter ships, and that focus might cost us our air superiority if we didn't focus on the battleships.

A report from Val came through next. "Warehouse is secure!" she nearly shouted with excitement. "I'm we're still looking through for the sword, but as soon as we find it I'll have someone sent up to you."

It was massive news, but I had to force down my excitement as I was still busy with my command of the *Boston*. All I was able to afford was a short affirmative.

By now the first of the Skydrifters were close enough to be in range of our smaller weapons, so I diverted yet more power away from the main canon to give those juice and also to power our thrusters for when we needed to maneuver. After that, I spoke up over the ship's PA system: "All gunners, you may fire at will."

Lasers, torpedos, and plasma bursts began criss-crossing the expanse as both fleets opened fire. For some reason, though, the Skydrifters were focusing their fire on the *Boston*, at the expense of any harassment of the rest of our fleet. A new tactic Cubism had thought up? It wasn't a very clever one. I simply drew as much of the *Boston*'s power as I could to the shields, disarming the ship. The entire Skydrifter fleet could barely beat through this power output, and our shielding was trickling down only slowly, a tenth of a percent a time. Nevertheless, the *Boston* was rocked by vibrations from absorbing the incoming energy with its shields. Meanwhile, Jeremy, continuing with his

208

approach of reckless aggression, seemed to have dropped his shields entirely once he'd noticed this pattern, and the *Los Angeles* was putting out devastating amounts of damage.

I did flag my First Officer to inform Marissa to keep Kai on the surface, though. It seemed stupid to move the sword to the only ship Cubism had his forces shooting at.

My fleet disabled their first target, a destroyer that had been pulling up alongside the *Boston*. What was Cubism's game here? He wasn't making any meaningful progress, while we were putting his ships down one by one. It became clear once I remembered to look down at the surface of Carthas. His transports were dropping towards the surface for a ground assault, and the destroyer that we'd taken out had achieved its goal: a number of planetcrash pods had been launched from its underbelly, directly at Marissa's base on the surface. I was the one who was supposed to be holding this location, yet forced to focus all my power on defenses, I was unable to prevent the Skydrifters from launching their land assault. Cubism was playing the objective and the objectives were on the ground.

A Skydrifter frigate got close enough to give the *Boston* a broadside before the fleet could finish it off. Our shielding hit 90%. A tenth of a percent drop didn't seem like much, but as the enemy attacks just kept coming, it was starting to add up. I was losing shielding faster than Cubism was losing ships. If the *Boston* was destroyed up here, all the items we'd worked so hard to collect would be scattered in the orbit of Carthas.

I called my First Officer over from his station, across the bridge.

"Yes ma'am?"

"I'm needed planetside. You have the bridge."

"Yes, ma'am."

I started to walk towards the planetcrash pods, then hesitated. What kind of commanding officer didn't even bother to learn her second's name? "I never caught your name."

"I go by Grendel, ma'am."

"Grendel." I paused again, and handed him the transceiver I'd used to keep track of Marissa and Val. It wouldn't be useful if I was already on the ground with them. "Thank you."

He nodded solemnly and took the captain's chair. It was a long, quiet walk down to the pod, giving me plenty of time to second-guess myself. Was abandoning ship really the right call? Could there be something I was missing, some aspect of the situation I'd failed to consider? Despite my misgivings, as I walked, the rational part of my brain was unable to come up with any reason to stay. So when I arrived finally at the pods, I hesitated only for a moment before stepping in and launching myself to Marissa's base camp on the surface of Carthas.

My planetcrash was likely as violent as any I'd done before, but it felt strangely peaceful. The shaking on reentry was no worse than I'd been experiencing back on the *Boston*, but now I wasn't surrounded by gunfire. Instead of the adrenaline rush I usually felt on planetcrash, calmness descended over me as I descended to Carthas, a calmness that, outside of when I was with Ezra, I hadn't felt since splitting from Cubism.

And then the impact threw me back into a world of stress. I spent a few moments staying still in my pod, unable to move, to do anything except for hyperventilate. All at once, my paralysing rush of panic passed as soon as it had come.

I ejected from the pod and surveyed Marissa's base of operations. Or rather, what was left of it. Intense fighting raged around the bombed-out shell of our headquarters, with bullets and lasers streaking overhead. It was incredible how fast the Skydrifters had destroyed it. Presumably one of their ships had taken some potshots from orbit.

Another pod slammed into the ground near me, sending a wave of mud flying through the air in all directions. I scrambled into cover and equipped my rifle, ready to fire if its passenger proved to be a Skydrifter. But no: it had the Artemis insignia on the exterior, which I could see now that the mud had settled. I lowered my rifle and out came…

"Jeremy?"

"Oh, thank God," he said. "I was worried I was gonna miss you."

"Why are you down here?"

"Followed you down when I heard you'd evac'd. I thought I should be with you for the end. Did they find Asha?"

"Not that I've heard. Let's get to the warehouse first, pick up Kai."

He nodded and we dashed off through the mud. It was nighttime on the surface, so we were unafraid of being seen as we trekked through the landscape. The fighting had spread out from Marissa's base, and we passed skirmishes from time to time as we moved, giving them extra breadth so avoid getting sucked into the battles. We had a more important mission to run.

As we continued, Grendel called me with a status update from the naval battle above us.

"Report quickly, I'm a little busy down here."

"If you want to save the *Boston*, we'll have to evacuate now." He paused. "But I believe we should stay on, and the bridge crew is with me. The enemy is diverting valuable resources eliminating us, and I believe we can win this battle if we sacrifice the *Boston*."

He was probably right. In my last few minutes aboard the vessel, I'd seen how we could grind out victories even against Cubism's flagships so long as they focused on the *Boston*. All the same, it was a noble sacrifice by the crew.

211

"Stay. And Grendel: tell the crew, on behalf of the whole faction, thank you."

"Aye aye, ma'am." He ended the call. I indulged a moment to look upward at the battle, watching the massive ships in low orbit fight for our future.

Our caution paid off, and we arrived at the warehouse without incident. The hole Val had blown in its wall was even more impressive when I could view it in person and I was enormously glad that she hadn't accidentally destroyed Kai.

I stepped inside and got my first look past the rubble from the explosion. Bodies littered the floor, both Skydrifters and Artemis marines. My heart stopped when I realized who was among them. Marissa and Val lay dead in the center of the floor.

Without warning, Jeremy pushed me to the ground, pressing his shotgun to the back of my head. "Don't. Move." he growled.

From the staircase up to the warehouse roof, a squad of Skydrifter marines descended, rifles all aimed at me. Behind them, holding both Asha and Kai, walked Cubism.

"Surprise!" Cubism called down cheerfully. "You fell for it!"

"I'm sorry," Jeremy said, quieter now. "I had to."

"Why?" I asked.

"I couldn't let Cubism lose his father the way I lost mine. You don't know what that feels like, but I do. I won't let anyone else have to face that, not if I can help it. And if you want to stand in the way...I'll fight you. Or anyone else."

"So you were the leak, then. The one person I told everything, you were always on his side."

"Right from the beginning. He talked to me before you did, persuaded me to go along with you."

I cursed.

212

"We didn't even bother collecting items, once you formed your little Artemis club," Cubism chimed in. "You did all that for us! Now with these two"—he waved Kai and Asha—"all we need to do is kill you and take everything else off your body!"

Cubism walked in close and laid the swords on my shoulders, Kai on my left and Asha on my right. "I'll do you the courtesy of killing you with these. You came all this way for them, after all."

He moved and the screen went black.

```
GAME OVER

Create new character? y/n
```

CHAPTER 34

No! This couldn't be happening! Having come so far, thrown my life off so much, just to fail? I smashed "y," bringing the character creation screen back up. I knew it was hopeless, but damn it, I wasn't going to give up!

The space battle must have turned in our favor: they'd sacrificed a massive fleet to eliminate me. If we could stop Cubism from using the exploit, maybe with orbital bombardment, he'd find it almost impossible to make a comeback.

I clicked through the character creation as fast as possible, not bothering to change anything from the defaults. I spawned back on Almanac, the planet for new characters. Immediately, I started to look for a ship, anything that could get me back onto Carthas.

Before I could find one though, the screen went black again. A message from the developers appeared.

```
Hey PlanetCrash players!

Someone just tried to hack the game,
exploiting a vulnerability we used to have
with how we handled payment information as
well as the ability to inject code onto our
server with item builds. We apologize for the
existence of these security issues and any
stress they may have caused.

Fortunately for us (and for your financial
info), user EDG2051 posted about this in the
```

214

forums to try to recruit an army to stop anyone from executing on that vulnerability.

(We do read the forums, after all.)

These issues were patched out shortly after, during the "routine maintenance" patch and server downtime of June 22.

Why are we only announcing this now?

We've never seen this behavior in a server before. Near total polarization between two warring factions has been unheard of in PlanetCrash's history. It would have been a shame to end that, especially once nothing was at stake after our patch.

We hope you enjoyed the war! The NA-22 server will be shut down for a few days and all characters will be reset on relaunch. We're giving a do-over to this server. All participants will get a permanent medal added to their profiles, marking them as participants in the largest war in PlanetCrash history, as well as a special victory medal for those associated with the Artemis alliance. Well played!

See you on relaunch!

PlanetCrash Development Team

It seemed so obvious, now. There had been hundreds of comments on my forum post, arguing about whether the exploit was real or not. Of course *someone* from the studio had seen it, and once they saw it, it only made sense that they'd check up on their security.

I slumped back in my chair. It was finally over, for good.

I closed *PlanetCrash* and opened the forums, curious to see what the reactions to this would be. My inbox was more full

215

than it ever had been, bursting with messages from people who'd seen my forum name in the message and reached out.

One of the items stood out though: it was from the official *PlanetCrash* account. I was surprised to see that it addressed me by my real name.

```
Emily,

We wanted to thank you personally for your
tireless effort to defend PlanetCrash and its
community. Thanks to you, both your fellow
players and the studio averted a catastrophe.

As a token of our thanks, we're inviting you
to come visit our offices and take a full
tour.

Beyond which, we've been looking for a
community manager lately. You have
qualifications we could only dream of: a
passion for the game, dedication to its
community, and trust already built between you
and many of the other players. We'd be
thrilled if you could take this role, perhaps
part-time at first while you finish school.

Let us know if you're interested.

Thank you again,

Edith Dowd, Creative Director of PlanetCrash
```

I wasn't sure I wanted anything to do with *PlanetCrash* for a long while. But it would have been stupid to reject the offer so soon, so I left it in my inbox without responding.

I logged out of the forums, then the computer I was at, returning my mind to the library, and the real-world Boston. I'd spent so much time at the library before the war had kept me cooped up in the SHU that I knew the way back down to the street like the back of my hand. But instead of going down to the side entrance, my usual exit, I took an unusual turn. The

216

front half of the library was the classic building from when it had originally been built, rather than the modern half where the teen area and computers lived. Something in my head was telling me to walk through it today. I admired the stone architecture as I went, and the fountain in the courtyard, art that I'd previously always just walked past without giving any consideration to.

Once I reached the front entrance and walked outside onto the stairs that led up to it, I paused to enjoy the warm summer day. I closed my eyes and appreciated the feeling of the sun on my face and arms.

After a few minutes of letting my mind blankly feel the world around me, freed finally, permanently, from the stress of trying to stop Cubism, I turned to walk towards the monorail station. It was time to go home.

I hesitated, though. Without even thinking, I'd headed back towards the SHU. Should I go back to my parents instead? Was I ready for that? My heart rate rose again, even considering the idea. I needed to talk it over with someone first. With Ezra. Back to the SHU it was.

Ezra wasn't there when I arrived, probably because he was still at work. I waited for him in the cafeteria, taking the opportunity to eat. I hadn't gotten the opportunity yet today, having rushed to the library immediately after waking.

I went back for seconds, then thirds, becoming acutely aware of the hunger that I'd been pushing aside for so long.

Ezra came in while I was still eating, flashing me a smile as he passed to grab his own dinner before coming back to sit across from me.

"It's over," I told him. "We won."

"Oh, thank God," he sighed. I wasn't sure whether he was referring to the people whose money we'd saved or that I was

217

out of *PlanetCrash*. He paused for a moment. "Tell me what happened."

I recounted the day's events. It sunk in as I was talking that I'd just fought in, and lead, what was probably the largest battle in the history of *PlanetCrash*. It had been awe-inspiring, even though I'd been too stressed to appreciate it at the time. I fell silent for a moment. Probably right now, thousands of players would be uploading their footage of the battle to the internet, with millions more tuning in to watch from other servers, and likely other gaming communities as well.

I ended my story with the job offer I'd received.

"You're taking that, right?" Ezra asked.

"Honestly, I don't know. I'm just exhausted with *Planet-Crash* lately."

"Emily, this is an incredible opportunity for you. You've never wanted that 'normal' stuff, go to school and all that. This is a way for you to make your way without doing that."

He was right. From that perspective, taking the job was a no-brainer. "Yeah. I just…need a break first."

"Totally understandable. But write back and tell them that instead of leaving them hanging."

I nodded. "I'll do that."

Erza eyed me. "Do it now. You want to show that you're on top of things. Always helps to make a good first impression on your employer."

Smiling, I put my hands up in mock defeat. "I'll do it now," I said, chuckling as I stood up to go back to my room and compose a response. "Talk to you in the morning?"

"I don't have work tomorrow, so don't worry about waking up early or anything," he replied, laughing as well. "Catch you then."

218

When I got back to my room, I reopened the *PlanetCrash* forums to reread the message they'd sent me.

```
We'd be thrilled if you could take this role,
perhaps part-time at first while you finish
school.
```

I'd forgotten to mention that last proposal to Ezra. It made the offer less exciting, having to keep going to class and the implication hung over the message that if I quit school they wouldn't simply shift me to full-time. But even with that, I'd spent a good amount of my life going to school and playing *PlanetCrash* after getting home in the evenings. This would mean getting that life back, only getting paid for it as well. It would be a sweet gig, assuming *PlanetCrash* could ever again be as fun as it had been before Cubism had changed it for me.

Even if it never got back to that, though, this was still as good of a job as I could hope for, so I set to writing my reply.

```
Edith,

Thank you so much for the offer! I'd be
thrilled to work at PlanetCrash Studios. I
don't know what you were thinking for a start
date, but if it's acceptable I'd like to take
some time before starting. I've been putting a
lot of hours into PlanetCrash as a result of
this situation, and now that it's over I want
to take a break from the game and spend some
time with my family. Let me know if this is
okay on your end.

Thank you again for the opportunity to work at
PlanetCrash Studios,

Emily Wilson
```

I slept like a baby that night, waking up only when it was almost noon. Ezra wasn't in the cafeteria when I got down there, so I ate quickly before heading back up to his room on the third floor.

His door was open. He must have been expecting me. I stepped inside, looking around at his room. I'd never been inside before. It wasn't too different from my room: a cot, blank beige walls, and a small closet.

Ezra was looking at something on his phone and hadn't noticed me enter.

"Hey," I said.

"Oh, hi," he replied, looking up and sliding his phone back into his pocket. "When I said you didn't have to worry about waking up early…you really took that to heart." He smiled at me.

I smiled back, a little guiltily. "Sorry, man, I just haven't been getting enough sleep lately, what with—"

"I know," Ezra said, cutting me off. "I'm just kidding."

"Ezra…" I shifted uncomfortably, not sure how to say what I had to next. "I'm going home today. Like, back to my parents."

"Good," he replied. "I've liked having you around, but honestly you shouldn't be here."

"Are you going to be okay with…" I gestured around vaguely. "Everything?"

"Emily, I'll be fine. Go home; don't worry about me." He reached for a piece of paper that sat on his cot and offered it to me. "In case you want to stay in touch, though."

I took it. "Thank you."

I was surprised to realize, as I walked away, how much I'd grown attached to Ezra in the time I'd spent in the SHU. Of course, I'd still be able to see him: I'd already entered his number, written on the paper he'd given me, into my phone. But it

220

wouldn't be possible anymore to just hang out on such short notice any night.

I considered stopping by Jeremy's house before going to my parents, as it was within walking distance and arguing over his decision to hand me over to Cubism, but I ultimately rejected the idea. He'd betrayed me, hurt me, and I didn't want anything more to do with him. No, I'd go home.

A few minutes later I was back on the Red Line train, headed back to my parents' home in Jamaica Plain. I nearly missed the transfer in to the Orange Line since I'd grown so accustomed to riding to the library and nowhere else. It was another reminder of how much Cubism and *PlanetCrash* had dominated my life over the past months.

Disembarking back in JP was strange, after having been gone for so long. Everything felt new and familiar at the same time. The things that had changed, a repainted house here, new graffiti there, stood out to me, breaking from my memory of what had been. My parents' house, though, looked the same. The faded red paint on the front steps, the place where the porch handrail was broken. Nothing had changed, as far as I could tell. But it still felt different somehow.

I summoned my courage, and knocked on the front door. Mom answered the door a moment later. She dropped the glass she'd been holding when she saw me, which fell to the carpet and spilled her wine. I watched the dark stain spread, suddenly aware that I didn't know what to say.

Mom pulled me into a hug before I could say anything, holding me tightly to her. I put my arms around her. "Hi," I muttered lamely into her shoulder.

"I'm so glad you're home," Mom whispered.

"You're not mad?" I asked.

"I was," she replied. "I was scared at first, then mad, but eventually that all went away. I just wanted you home."

"I'm home now. And I'm sorry. I should never have left."

Eventually Mom let go, and we sat down at the kitchen table together. She called dad downstairs and I told them what had happened. Why I'd left, how I'd discovered that Cubism had fooled me, and how I'd stopped him.

They were, inevitably, not impressed with what I'd done. I felt like in their minds, I'd just spent months playing a video game, wasting my life. But like Mom had said, their anger had faded in the time I'd been gone, and I didn't have to bear the brunt of it. Besides which, the revelation that I'd been offered a job at *PlanetCrash* Studios seemed to assuage their fears about me "throwing my future away."

That said, this attitude didn't bother me the way it used to. They had a point, after all. If I'd told my parents about Cubism's plan when it was first pitched to me, they'd have said it was too good to be true. I'd known that then, and I still knew it now. But now I also knew that they were right.

Despite what I'd told Mom and Dad, though, I had no regrets. For all the stress, the mistakes, the lack of sleep, Jeremy's betrayal...all of it had been an experience that I'd never had before and likely never would again. I wouldn't want to give that up even if I'd had the opportunity.

Once I was back home, it was almost eerie how quickly my life returned to normalcy. School was supposed to restart only a few weeks later. I'd have to repeat a year since I'd missed so much of it, but that honestly was a benefit: I could start again with a new class that didn't know me, which would likely prevent any rumors from taking off. It wasn't like I'd had lots of friends in my old grade that I'd miss.

My job at PlanetCrash Studios was supposed to start a month after school did, at the end of September. That suited me fine, giving me plenty of time to mentally refresh from my *PlanetCrash* burnout. I took the time before the start of classes to catch up on reading, diving back into books I'd neglected for far too long. When school restarted, though, the *PlanetCrash* itch came back, and I started playing again after school. Though, since my job was dependent on staying in class, I put in more effort than I had before and my grades rose a bit.

All this meant that by the time my first day rolled around, I was incredibly excited to begin.

CHAPTER 35

PlanetCrash Studios' Boston office was actually located in Cambridge, so I grabbed the Red Line after my final class of the day.

The tour Edith gave when I arrived was a little underwhelming. Sure, there were a few cool *PlanetCrash* artifacts around, but at the end of the day it was an office building. It did seem like a fine place to work, though, which I was happy about. The free food they provided was a huge plus.

When she finished, Edith brought me to my office. "This is where you'll be sitting." She gestured around. "HR has some paperwork they need you to fill out for onboarding, and they'll bring it here. Feel free to chill, get used to it, whatever, while you wait."

"Thanks," I replied.

"Any questions before I leave you to it?" she asked.

"Do you know what happened to Cubism? Was he telling the truth about his dad being sick?"

Edith shrugged, "I honestly don't know. We don't know who he is. He paid for server entrance using a prepaid debit card, and the account wasn't active on any other servers. If you have any ideas about how to find him, I'm all ears. But I don't expect it to go anywhere. We banned his account, and as far as I'm concerned, that's the end of it. If he comes back, we'll deal with him then."

I nodded. "I'll keep an eye out, but knowing him, he'll make himself hard to find."

She turned to leave, then turned back. "I can't believe I forgot to mention: we're working on a prequel to *PlanetCrash*, which we're calling *PlanetRise*. We don't have the pre-alpha build installed on your computer yet, but remind me when I'm free and we'll get it for you. As long as you promise to let us know what you think, of course."

"That's awesome! I'd love to give feedback."

"I'm sure you would," she laughed. "But try to remember that your primary job is with *PlanetCrash* for now."

"Of course," I replied. "You don't have to tell me twice."

"Great," she said. "I'll leave you to it." With that, she stepped out of my office, lightly closing the door behind her.

I sat down at the chair they'd given me—a far more comfortable one than I'd had at the library or at home—and thought about what Edith had said. A prequel to *PlanetCrash*? It was incredibly exciting. I spent a few minutes wondering what would change, and what exactly was meant by the title *PlanetRise*. Would it be a mechanic in the game like PlanetCrash had been?

After a few minutes, though, this train of thought just instilled an intense desire to play *PlanetCrash*, so I booted up the PC under my desk. It must have been a beast under its rather unassuming hood, as it had the fastest boot time I'd ever seen. It made sense, given the job, but I still hadn't been ready for it.

What I did expect was *PlanetCrash* to be already installed as default software, and sure enough it was. I launched the game and logged into my account. Marissa and Val were both online, as they tended to be on Friday afternoons, so I invited each of them to my party. Both accepted the invite within a minute.

The server reset had taken away the majority of our equipment and experience, of course. We were down to a single

225

small corvette to transport the three of us around, but we weren't fighting epic battles lately. Mostly we were pursuing quests and messing around. It was the least seriously I'd ever taken *PlanetCrash*, and I'd been having a blast.

They spawned into our corvette, named the *Boston* in honor of my flagship in Artemis, and I greeted them. After about a minute of catching up on their days, I pulled up the galaxy map for all of us to see.

"So," I asked. "Where to now?"

ABOUT THE AUTHOR

Matthew Boudreau is a science fiction, fantasy, and gamelit author living in the New York City metro area, who began writing when he was eight because that was what his older sister did. When not writing about the robots in his head, he is an engineer who can be found working on the robots in his hands.